A Heart's Investment -

Dear Reader,

Thank you for picking up A Heart's Investment - Beyond Billions. In your hands, you hold a story that, while undeniably sprinkled with wealth, opulence, and all the luxuries you could imagine, is truly about discovering something much rarer and infinitely more valuable. This book isn't just a tale about money; it's a journey—a sometimes bumpy, often hilarious path from material wealth to the kind that can't be counted or bought.

Our protagonist, Leo Masters, is the quintessential billionaire who seemingly has it all: the palatial estate, the world-renowned status, and perhaps a collection of sports cars that would rival a small country's GDP. But, as Leo finds out (and as we might, too, if we had his fortune), all the riches in the world can't buy the deep happiness that comes from human connection, purpose, and giving back.

I wrote this story to explore a question I think we've all asked ourselves at one point or another: What does it truly mean to be wealthy? Is it a figure in a bank account, or is it something more? As Leo navigates his lavish, money-driven world and slowly stumbles—sometimes awkwardly, sometimes humorously—into acts of kindness and self-discovery, he starts to see that true wealth might not be about accumulation but about connection, purpose, and legacy.

You'll laugh, hopefully, as you follow Leo's not-so-graceful steps into a life of deeper meaning. You'll encounter moments of drama and genuine warmth as he grapples with a world he's known all his life and one he's just beginning to understand. Above all, I hope you'll see that each of us has a "heart investment" waiting for us—something or someone worth pouring ourselves into, even if it doesn't yield dividends in cash but rather in smiles, gratitude, and joy.

So join me as we step into Leo's world. May his journey inspire a bit of reflection and perhaps a few hearty laughs along the way. And maybe, just maybe, you'll find that you, too, have more wealth in your life than you ever realized.

Here's to investing in what really matters!
Warmest regards,
Smita Singh

A Heart's Investment - Beyond Billions

Smita Singh

Published by Smita Singh, 2024.

This is a work of fiction. Similarities to real people, places, or events are entirely coincidental.

A HEART'S INVESTMENT - BEYOND BILLIONS

First edition. October 28, 2024.

Copyright © 2024 Smita Singh.

ISBN: 979-8227814517

Written by Smita Singh.

Chapter 1: The Bottom Line Mirage

Chapter 2: The Golden Bubble

Chapter 3: The Awkward Charity Gala

Chapter 4: The Unpaid Smile

Chapter 5: High Stakes, Low Impact

Chapter 6: The Tax Write-Off

Chapter 7: The Money Can't Fix Everything Moment

Chapter 8: The Unmarketable Smile

Chapter 9: The Currency of Kindness

Chapter 10: The Lost Profit

Chapter 11: The Silver Lining Trade

Chapter 12: The Value of Nothing

Chapter 13: The Real Estate of the Heart

Chapter 14: The Debt of Gratitude

Chapter 15: The Final Investment

Chapter 1: The Bottom Line Mirage

Leo Masters woke up, not to a sunlit morning or a gentle alarm, but to the precise chime of his custom-made wake-up app, programmed to sound exactly at 5:00 AM. Every day. He'd read somewhere that consistency was key to success, and he lived by it religiously. Leo wasn't the type to hit the snooze button. Time, after all, was money. And if there was one thing Leo valued above all, it was the bottom line.

The billionaire's morning routine was as refined as a five-star menu. With no time to waste, Leo began his day by monitoring his stock portfolio on three separate screens—because why risk trusting just one when billions were at stake? This was his form of "morning meditation": a ritual of numbers, tickers, and quick calculations that kept him grounded in what he called *reality*. But in a strange twist, Leo's reality was more like a carefully managed performance, polished and optimized to the decimal point.

Leo's penthouse in the heart of the city was the epitome of luxury, furnished with custom-made furniture, art collections that would make museums jealous, and a kitchen equipped with more gadgets than a sci-fi spaceship. And yet, his place felt strangely devoid of life. The air was thick with an odd emptiness, one that not even the scent of his ultra-premium coffee could mask. Every morning, as he watched his coffee brew—timed down to the exact second for the perfect flavor—he would mentally tick off every aspect of his life that fit his "profitability matrix."

For Leo, everything had to fit into this matrix, and it wasn't limited to business decisions. He calculated the most efficient way to walk from his bedroom to his bathroom. He once timed the exact seconds it took for his elevator to reach the lobby—14 seconds, on average—and then had the elevator adjusted to shave off 0.5 seconds by upgrading to faster sensors. Time, after all, was precious.

As he sipped his coffee, Leo reflected on his day ahead: meetings with investors, a lunch with a potential merger partner, and an evening spent at a gala (sponsorship potential in mind, of course). Life was just one big, carefully managed spreadsheet for Leo. And yet, behind his witty commentary on the minutiae of his routine, there was a subtle hint of dissatisfaction. Each event on his schedule served a purpose—a deal to be closed, a connection to be made—but not a single moment was just *for him*.

Leo's friends—or rather, his "associates," as he preferred to call them—would often marvel at his success. He'd managed to become one of the wealthiest people in the country, self-made, from nothing to everything, building his empire from the ground up. But they couldn't see what lay behind his perfectly curated image. For Leo, life was a game of numbers, statistics, and calculated outcomes. Emotions? They were merely distractions.

At meetings, Leo was famously unflappable. He'd perfected the art of looking attentive while mentally running complex financial models, always calculating the potential return on investment of each conversation. During one particularly long-winded pitch from a junior executive, he once mused about how much money he could save if he charged a "wasted time" fee. Yet, despite his sharp humor, he never laughed. Not really. His smirks and raised eyebrows were simply part of his arsenal, used to convey a sense of charm and gravitas.

To the outside world, Leo was a powerhouse, admired for his cold precision. Yet behind closed doors, his solitary existence was marked by routines so meticulous they verged on absurd. His life was scripted like a business plan, with every moment dedicated to maximizing returns. While he presented an image of sophistication and poise, Leo had started feeling a subtle sense of something missing, something he couldn't quite name.

Leo had grown up with modest means, and perhaps that was the seed of his obsession with financial success. His childhood home was filled with love but short on luxuries, and he'd watched his parents struggle to make ends meet. He had vowed to be different. But now, with his success far surpassing anything he could have imagined, he felt a gnawing dissatisfaction.

His office was a testament to his achievements, with floor-to-ceiling windows overlooking the city skyline. Yet, even this grand view didn't spark joy. Each time he looked out, he merely noted the value of his real estate holdings in the surrounding blocks. People envied him, but Leo often wondered what there was to envy. His life was filled with status symbols, yet empty of the laughter and spontaneity he saw in others—qualities he'd long since written off as luxuries of the *unfocused*.

After the market closed that afternoon, Leo found himself doing something unusual: he decided to take a walk. Not a power walk, not a quick dash from one high-rise to another, but a real, aimless walk. As he strolled through the city streets, a rare sense of nostalgia crept in. He remembered his early days, those wild, unpredictable times when every dollar counted, and every small victory was celebrated with unbridled joy. Back then, he didn't need high-end suits or a penthouse view to feel successful. Just a simple cup of coffee after a good deal was enough to make him feel like he was on top of the world.

Just as Leo was turning to head back to his penthouse, he spotted an old friend, Tom, a high school buddy he hadn't seen in years. Tom was hardly recognizable in his mismatched clothes, unkempt hair, and a grin so wide it seemed almost out of place in the polished city streets.

"Leo! It's been ages!" Tom shouted, oblivious to the stares of onlookers. Leo, uncharacteristically unsure, managed a small smile, trying to keep the conversation short. But Tom wasn't one for subtlety, and before he knew it, Leo was dragged into a nearby coffee shop, seated at a tiny, wobbly table that was worlds apart from his usual mahogany conference tables.

They talked, and to Leo's surprise, Tom didn't care about his latest acquisition or the value of his company's stock. Instead, Tom spoke passionately about his family, his work as a school teacher, and his latest attempt to teach his kids "the wonders of an analog life." Leo listened with a mix of amusement and envy, especially as Tom recounted stories about his young daughter's school project on "How to save the world with kindness." It was utterly unprofitable, completely devoid of investment potential, yet Tom spoke with such genuine happiness that Leo couldn't help but listen.

"Remember when we were kids?" Tom mused, leaning back with a wistful grin. "We had big dreams. Not just big bank accounts."

"Those were simpler times," Leo replied, his tone as neutral as ever. But something in him stirred, as if those memories were trying to remind him of something he'd long forgotten.

That night, back in his penthouse, Leo poured himself a glass of his most expensive scotch, as he did every evening, and settled into his usual chair. He checked his watch, noting the exact second the liquid touched his lips. But the smooth burn, which once gave him a sense of accomplishment, now felt hollow. The view from his windows, the luxurious surroundings, and even the meticulously selected artwork on his walls felt like part of a set piece—grand, beautiful, but curiously empty.

For the first time, he allowed himself to ask a question that had been lurking in the back of his mind: *What's all this for?*

Days passed, and Leo's thoughts kept drifting back to his conversation with Tom. The idea that happiness could be found in things other than profit, power, and status felt both absurd and strangely alluring. On a whim, he decided to explore this notion—after all, he reasoned, sometimes even an investment needed fresh perspective.

So, Leo began to seek out small moments, things that didn't fit neatly into his bottom line. He started by reading a book, something entirely unrelated to finance or productivity—just a novel that Tom had recommended. Then, one afternoon, he decided to try out a café that wasn't his usual, opting for a crowded, bustling shop filled with chatter and laughter. The coffee was ordinary, the seating uncomfortable, yet he couldn't deny he felt a sense of connection, watching people around him sharing stories, laughing, and celebrating life in a way he hadn't felt in years.

These small changes didn't yield immediate results in his "happiness quotient," as he sarcastically called it, but they left a lingering feeling of curiosity. He began to suspect that perhaps his relentless pursuit of the bottom line had distracted him from something more profound.

In a twist of fate, Leo found himself facing a challenging decision at work: a proposal to automate certain operations in one of his companies, which would mean layoffs for hundreds of employees. Normally, he wouldn't hesitate, focusing solely on the numbers, but this time, a memory of Tom's words—"big dreams, not just big bank accounts"—resurfaced.

For the first time, Leo questioned his own decisions. He realized that his "bottom line" approach had created a mirage, an illusion of success built on relentless profit and power but devoid of human connection or compassion. He'd once believed that wealth was his ultimate achievement, but now, faced with the prospect of impacting people's lives, he wondered if there wasn't something greater than his bank balance.

Leo's story was just beginning, yet he could already sense a change within himself. This wasn't an overnight transformation; it was merely the start of a journey toward rediscovering what truly mattered. As he looked out at the city skyline from his penthouse, the lights that once symbolized his achievements now held a different meaning. Somewhere beyond the gleaming towers and financial reports, a new path was emerging—one where wealth wasn't measured in numbers, but in the lives he could touch.

Chapter 2: The Golden Bubble

Leo Masters lived in a golden bubble, a bubble of luxury and exclusivity that not only protected him from discomfort but also distanced him from the realities that shaped the lives of most people. This "bubble" wasn't just a metaphor; it was a finely tuned ecosystem tailored to make his life as seamless as possible. From the smart home that automatically brewed his coffee at exactly 74 degrees to the personal assistant who scheduled every minute of his day, Leo's world functioned on invisible gears he rarely, if ever, noticed.

Within his bubble, every whim was a command. If he had a craving for imported Colombian mangoes, they would arrive at his penthouse within an hour. His chauffeur, Robert, was a stoic, unflappable professional who anticipated Leo's moods like clockwork. The bubble was so all-encompassing that, for Leo, interactions with the "outside world" were an occasional, almost exotic rarity. But as fate would have it, a seemingly trivial event would soon expose him to the nuances of life outside his bubble—a life he had long since forgotten.

The day began as usual, with Leo going through his meticulously planned morning ritual. As he sipped his coffee, Leo received a notification from his assistant that Robert, his loyal chauffeur, had fallen ill and wouldn't be able to drive him to his morning meeting. Leo read the message with disbelief.

"What do you mean, Robert's sick?" he muttered, staring at his phone as if it were malfunctioning.

"Yes, sir," his assistant responded over the phone. "He called in this morning. I'm terribly sorry; I know this is unexpected."

Leo blinked. He hadn't dealt with such a trivial problem in years. "Can't you find a substitute?"

"Unfortunately, all our backup drivers are currently occupied," his assistant replied apologetically. "I've arranged for a car service, and they'll arrive in fifteen minutes."

Leo felt a pang of irritation. A car service? Wasn't that something other people used? The very idea felt uncomfortable, almost invasive. Yet he had no choice. A new sense of trepidation crept in as he realized he'd be, for the first time in a long time, entering unfamiliar territory. The thought of a stranger's car, not pre-programmed to his preferences, seemed oddly daunting.

When the car arrived, Leo approached it with hesitant curiosity. It wasn't the usual polished, impeccably silent luxury vehicle he was used to but rather an ordinary sedan, clean yet undeniably plain. The driver, an older gentleman with a friendly smile and an open demeanor, greeted Leo as he got in.

"Good morning, Mr. Masters!" the driver said warmly. "I'll be taking you to your destination today."

Leo nodded curtly, thrown by the driver's friendliness. Robert never spoke unless spoken to, and even then, his responses were brief and business-like. This driver, however, didn't seem bound by such protocol.

As they merged into city traffic, Leo felt uneasy. The ride was...normal. He hadn't realized just how accustomed he'd become to an unbreakable silence during his commutes. Here, the sounds of city life filtered through the car windows: honking horns, street vendors, and the occasional blare of a siren. It was distracting, almost chaotic, and he instinctively reached for the climate controls, only to realize with dismay that there was no panel at his side. He'd have to ask the driver.

Clearing his throat, Leo attempted to mask his discomfort. "Excuse me, could you turn the air conditioning down to...uh, 20 degrees Celsius?"

The driver raised an eyebrow, looking amused. "Sure thing, Mr. Masters, but I can only adjust it in rough settings. It's not the fancy climate control you're used to."

Leo chuckled awkwardly, pretending to find the situation funny, though it was anything but. How did people survive in cars without precise temperature control?

The driver, seemingly oblivious to Leo's growing discomfort, continued with casual chitchat. "So, Mr. Masters, you must have a busy day ahead?"

Leo managed a polite nod, struggling to come up with a response. Small talk was foreign territory for him. After a few seconds of silence, he replied, "Yes... meetings...business deals... the usual."

The driver nodded knowingly, then proceeded to offer his own anecdotes about navigating traffic and the quirks of city life, sprinkling his comments with genuine enthusiasm that was, to Leo, both baffling and oddly endearing. As he listened, he realized the driver found joy in the smallest things—like finding a shortcut through the downtown area or scoring a free coffee from a barista he'd befriended over the years.

As they approached a crowded intersection, a pedestrian darted into the street, causing the driver to brake suddenly. Leo lurched forward, instinctively gripping the seat. In his world, things like sudden stops and jaywalkers simply didn't happen. He was unused to the small unpredictabilities that seemed to pepper the lives of ordinary people.

When the driver finally muttered an apology for the abrupt stop, Leo, still rattled, tried to compose himself. He shot an annoyed glance at the pedestrian, now safely on the sidewalk and completely oblivious to the chaos they'd caused. The incident left Leo shaken and with an uncomfortable realization: his bubble had shielded him from even the most mundane inconveniences of city life.

To calm his nerves, he pulled out his phone and attempted to order a coffee for pickup at his destination. But to his horror, his favorite coffee shop's app was undergoing maintenance. It was almost laughable how something as trivial as a coffee order could derail his sense of control.

"Sir," the driver said, breaking into Leo's thoughts. "There's a small café a few blocks down. They've got some of the best coffee around—better than those fancy places, if I do say so myself."

Ordinarily, Leo would have dismissed the suggestion without a second thought, but his options were limited, and the idea of experiencing "authentic" coffee was oddly enticing. He agreed, and they detoured to the café.

The café was a far cry from the sterile, upscale coffee shops Leo usually frequented. It was a cozy place with wooden tables, eclectic art on the walls, and the comforting smell of freshly brewed coffee. Leo, who hadn't set foot in a non-corporate establishment in years, felt like an anthropologist venturing into an uncharted culture.

Standing in line, he was visibly uncomfortable. People chatted and laughed, paying him no special attention. Accustomed to being treated with reverence, Leo was bewildered by the indifference. When his turn came, he glanced at the menu, which lacked the specificity he was used to. There were no options for oat milk or a half-sweet, double-shot latte. With a shrug, he ordered a simple black coffee and braced himself for the "unfiltered" taste.

When his coffee arrived, Leo took a sip, expecting the worst. But to his surprise, the rich flavor was actually...pleasant. Somehow, this humble café's coffee was more satisfying than the meticulously crafted, imported blends he usually consumed. It was simple, unpretentious, and grounding.

As he savored the unfamiliar taste, Leo overheard a conversation at a nearby table where two friends were discussing life's small joys and frustrations. One man was talking about his daughter's soccer game, where she'd accidentally scored for the opposing team but ended up laughing it off, unfazed. The other, a woman, shared her excitement about finally paying off her student loans. These weren't the kinds of stories he'd ever paid attention to before, yet there was a rawness and authenticity to them that left him oddly reflective.

With his coffee finished and no chauffeur to take him the rest of the way, Leo faced another unexpected ordeal: public transportation. His assistant had texted him directions to the nearest subway station, so, reluctantly, he made his way there. Descending into the bustling underground, Leo felt like he was entering a foreign country.

Navigating the subway map was a challenge. Used to apps that guided his every step, he found the lack of specificity maddening. He took a wrong turn and ended up on the wrong platform twice. By the time he finally boarded the correct train, he was sweating and frustrated, wedged between a college student with blaring headphones and an elderly woman clutching a knitting bag.

The train lurched forward, and Leo stumbled, grabbing a pole for support. He cast an awkward smile at the elderly woman, who responded with a warm grin and a remark about "city life." She then struck up a conversation, asking him if he took the subway often.

"Not... usually," he replied, to which she chuckled.

"Well, it's a grand adventure, isn't it?" she said with a twinkle in her eye.

Leo almost laughed, but something about her enthusiasm made him pause. The subway, an "adventure"? To him, it was a nightmare. Yet, her words echoed in his mind. This ordinary woman found joy in something he deemed beneath him.

When Leo finally arrived at his office, he was exhausted and slightly frazzled. The usual smooth efficiency of his routine had been replaced by unpredictability, and he was ready to retreat back into his bubble. But something about the day's encounters lingered in his thoughts. The driver's simple stories, the unpretentious coffee, the elderly woman's joyful embrace of the mundane—these experiences felt oddly refreshing, like glimpses into a world he'd long forgotten.

His pristine office now seemed sterile, devoid of the vibrancy he'd encountered outside. He sat at his desk, his mind drifting back to the conversations he'd overheard, the warm smile of the elderly woman, and the unfiltered taste of that black coffee. The numbers on his screen, once his primary source of satisfaction, felt somehow hollow in comparison.

As he glanced at the towering cityscape through his window, Leo felt a subtle but undeniable shift. The world beyond his bubble, with all its unpredictabilities and imperfections, held a richness he hadn't anticipated. A world he had carefully kept at bay had, in a single day, revealed itself to be far more complex, humorous, and surprisingly heartwarming than he'd ever imagined.

Chapter 3: The Awkward Charity Gala

Leo Masters prided himself on his professionalism. He kept his schedule packed, avoided any unnecessary risks, and meticulously built a life free of surprises. Yet, on this particular evening, Leo found himself wearing a tuxedo and sporting an uncomfortable smile as he stepped into an event he wanted no part in: the annual "Hope for Humanity" charity gala.

This wasn't his usual scene. Leo's idea of philanthropy was simple—donating precisely the minimum amount needed to maintain favorable PR and keep tax deductions on his side. He saw this gala as another transaction, a public relations maneuver to give his image a touch of warmth. But as he entered the opulent hall filled with crystal chandeliers, floral arrangements, and people he had absolutely no interest in, he quickly realized he was out of his depth.

The event was bustling, with guests elegantly dressed, mingling with easy laughter and champagne flutes in hand. Leo spotted a few familiar faces: people he'd met in business circles or seen in financial magazines. Yet, tonight, those people weren't discussing stock prices or market forecasts. They were engaged in serious conversations about "impact," "awareness," and "sustainable change"—topics that, for Leo, carried about as much meaning as the phrase "home-cooked meal."

His assistant, Fiona, had briefed him on the basics of the charity beforehand, though Leo had only half-listened, scrolling through emails during her speech. She'd mentioned something about their goal of providing clean water and education to underprivileged communities. Honestly, it all sounded noble but vague, just the usual fodder for wealthy patrons to pat themselves on the back.

As he wandered toward the champagne bar, Leo was stopped by a tall, enthusiastic woman with a clipboard in hand.

"Mr. Masters, thank you so much for joining us tonight! We are thrilled to have your support for Hope for Humanity."

Leo gave her a polite nod, realizing this was his cue to appear genuinely interested. He smiled, aiming for the level of warmth he had seen in the mirror that morning during his "charming billionaire" practice session. "Yes, well, it's... quite the cause," he replied, hoping he sounded sincere.

"Oh, absolutely!" she said, her eyes lighting up. "It's all thanks to people like you that we're able to make such a difference in people's lives."

Leo nodded, already half-regretting his decision to come. But he kept his facade intact, throwing in the occasional "Yes, indeed" and "Quite remarkable" as she rattled off statistics and accomplishments. Leo noted with a hint of despair that her enthusiasm showed no signs of slowing.

After what felt like an eternity of nodding, the woman finally mentioned a fundraiser that was being organized to build schools in rural villages across the globe. Leo wasn't listening fully—his eyes were drifting to the crowd, trying to identify the nearest exit. However, he nodded absentmindedly as she went on, a habit he regretted almost instantly.

"So, Mr. Masters," she continued excitedly, "how do you feel about our proposal? If we could count on your pledge, we're confident we can secure the entire project's funding."

Leo froze. Wait—did she just imply he was funding something? Surely he hadn't actually agreed to anything... right?

"Uh, yes... quite admirable work you're doing here," he stammered, trying to sidestep the conversation.

"Oh, thank you so much, Mr. Masters! With your generous pledge, we can start breaking ground by next spring," she beamed, her eyes almost sparkling with excitement.

Leo's smile wavered, but he tried to recover quickly. "Of course, happy to support, uh... all that."

"Oh, wonderful!" she exclaimed, patting him on the arm as if he were a benevolent deity blessing the crowd. "We'll make the official announcement after the keynote speech. Our entire team will be thrilled!"

As she walked away, Leo's brain scrambled to make sense of what had just happened. He had pledged something. Something big, from the sound of it. But how big was "big"? And more importantly, how was he supposed to get out of this?

Desperate for a distraction, Leo turned his attention to the guests around him. He quickly realized that the people attending this gala were worlds apart from his typical business associates. They spoke in animated tones about causes they were passionate about, recounting stories of volunteering trips and heartwarming anecdotes about children whose lives had changed because of their donations.

Standing alone with a champagne flute in hand, Leo felt like an alien. In an attempt to fit in, he approached a nearby couple deep in conversation, ready to showcase his "interest" in the cause.

"It's amazing, isn't it?" he said, injecting a note of enthusiasm he hoped sounded genuine.

The couple smiled politely. "Oh, yes," the woman replied, clearly warming to the topic. "My husband and I just returned from a trip to Ghana, where we worked on providing access to clean water in remote areas."

Leo felt a bead of sweat form at his temple. "Right, water. So important... hydration," he said, grasping for words and settling on the obvious.

The couple exchanged glances. The man nodded, trying to keep the conversation going. "Absolutely. Access to clean water is life-changing. It's not just about drinking; it affects health, education, and economic opportunities."

"Oh, definitely," Leo replied, nodding far too eagerly. "Water is... fundamental."

"Do you have any personal experiences in the field, Mr. Masters?" the woman asked, her tone curious.

Leo's heart skipped a beat. Personal experience? The closest he had come to a "cause" was having a particularly moving bottle of vintage wine from a remote region in France. But he couldn't very well say that. Clearing his throat, he opted for an exaggerated, vague answer.

"Well, you know, I... I've encountered my fair share of challenges," he said, trying to look contemplative. "And, uh, water is... one of the big ones."

The couple nodded, though their expressions hinted at mild confusion. Leo forced a smile, excused himself, and retreated to the buffet table. The entire event felt like a high-stakes game, and he was rapidly losing.

Soon, the lights dimmed, signaling the beginning of the keynote speech. Leo spotted the woman with the clipboard near the stage, sending him an enthusiastic thumbs-up. Leo felt a pang of dread. Was she really going to announce his "pledge"?

The speaker began with a story about how Hope for Humanity was founded, then moved on to recount specific projects, complete with slides of smiling children, clean water fountains, and newly constructed school buildings. Leo noticed the faces around him watching the presentation, expressions of genuine empathy etched on their faces. For the first time, he felt an odd flicker of something unfamiliar—a kind of curiosity about why these people cared so deeply.

"And now," the speaker continued, "we'd like to thank one of our most recent supporters, someone who's come forward tonight to help us build new schools for underprivileged children."

The crowd's attention sharpened. Leo could feel dozens of eyes on him, each one expecting him to stand up and graciously accept his role as a patron of the cause. The speaker gestured for him to join her on stage. Leo's heart pounded.

Awkwardly, he made his way to the stage, a forced smile plastered on his face. The applause was polite but genuine, and as he reached the microphone, he fumbled for something to say.

"Um, well, thank you all," he began, clearing his throat. "I'm honored to... support such an incredible organization."

The crowd nodded approvingly, and Leo, in his desperation, glanced down at the notes the speaker had left on the podium. Skimming through statistics and mission statements, he quickly read a line that struck him: *True wealth lies not in our bank accounts, but in the lives we touch.*

Pausing, Leo took a breath, then continued, almost surprising himself with the sincerity in his voice. "I have to admit," he said, his tone softer, "I came here tonight without really understanding what Hope for Humanity does. But seeing all of you here, hearing these stories... I realize that this organization truly changes lives."

The crowd murmured approvingly, and Leo felt his cheeks flush. He hadn't planned to say that. In fact, he hadn't planned to say much of anything. But, standing there in the spotlight, surrounded by people who genuinely cared, he realized his words weren't entirely false.

"To all of you who work tirelessly to make this world a better place," he finished, "thank you. I may be new to this, but I hope to... make a difference."

The applause was enthusiastic, and Leo quickly stepped off the stage, his heart pounding. He'd made it through, but the experience had shaken him more than he expected.

As he left the stage, guests approached him, commending his speech and thanking him for his generosity. Leo, still rattled, responded with awkward smiles and handshakes, unsure how to handle the praise. For the first time in his life, he felt as if he'd stepped into a world he didn't fully understand. It wasn't about assets or power plays; it was about something far deeper, something intangible.

And as he exited the gala, he couldn't shake the feeling that, despite the chaos, he'd glimpsed something real—a spark of purpose in a life he'd long considered perfectly complete.

Driving home, Leo replayed the night in his mind, alternating between embarrassment and a strange sense of accomplishment. Little did he know, his accidental pledge was about to change his life in ways he never could have imagined.

Chapter 4: The Unpaid Smile

Leo Masters had grown accustomed to certain reactions when he walked into a room: subtle glances, awed whispers, or the occasional direct approach from someone hoping to get close to his wealth. This time, though, the person who stood across from him in the dimly lit room of the Hope for Humanity volunteer headquarters showed no signs of awe. In fact, she looked almost... unimpressed.

She was leaning over a table, stacking boxes filled with supplies. Her hair was tied back in a messy bun, and her face bore the gentle lines of a life spent in the sun, without the fuss of high-end skincare routines. She wore a faded t-shirt and cargo pants, giving her an earthy, down-to-business vibe. Her name tag read "Grace," and she seemed totally engrossed in her work—until she looked up and noticed him standing there.

Grace's eyes flickered with brief curiosity, then she gave a small nod of acknowledgment, as though she were greeting a neighbor, and resumed her stacking.

"Well, hello," Leo said, adjusting his jacket. He was used to starting conversations, but this felt strange. He wasn't in a boardroom, and he wasn't there to close a deal. He was... volunteering. It felt foreign, like a strange new game.

Grace straightened up and gave him a friendly smile. "Hey, you must be the new guy," she said, extending her hand. "I'm Grace."

"Leo. Leo Masters," he replied, grasping her hand. He waited for the telltale spark of recognition, but there was nothing. No surprise, no awe, not even the faintest flicker of interest. Instead, she just nodded again.

"Great. We're lucky to have you. I hope you're ready to get your hands dirty," she said, gesturing toward a stack of supply boxes labeled "First Aid Kits."

Leo chuckled, brushing a bit of imaginary dust from his jacket. "I don't mind getting involved," he replied, hoping he sounded casual.

Grace smirked, glancing down at his spotless leather shoes. "We'll see."

As they began working, Leo quickly discovered he was out of his element. The boxes were heavier than they looked, and after just a few minutes, he could feel a faint but undeniable ache in his shoulders. Grace, on the other hand, moved through the tasks with practiced ease, tossing boxes to and fro, her hands calloused but steady.

"So," she said after a few moments, "what brings you to a place like this?"

Leo cleared his throat, stalling for time. He hadn't really planned an answer. "Well, I, uh, felt it was time to give back," he said, aiming for sincerity.

Grace raised an eyebrow, amusement flickering in her eyes. "Oh, really?" she asked, her tone light. "Not here to score a few PR points, then?"

Leo's cheeks warmed as he fumbled for a response. "I mean, I do believe in supporting worthy causes," he said defensively.

Grace's smile softened. "I'm just teasing you. We're grateful for every pair of hands we get. But it's funny... all these fancy people who come and go, talking about 'giving back' while making sure the cameras catch it. They never stick around long enough to really get involved."

Leo looked away, embarrassed, but her words stirred something uncomfortable in him. He'd grown accustomed to perfectly crafted lines, polished intentions, and image management. It was strange to be called out so openly.

Grace, however, seemed completely at ease, almost amused by his discomfort.

The day's tasks were simple but exhausting. By mid-afternoon, Leo found himself sneaking glances at his watch, estimating the hours he had left before he could retreat to his familiar comforts. As he was sorting through a pile of medical supplies, his phone buzzed with a notification.

Instinctively, he checked the screen. It was an alert from his stock portfolio. His hand paused, and his eyes quickly scanned the numbers, assessing the dip. His gaze narrowed, calculating potential implications, when a voice broke his concentration.

"What's that?" Grace asked, peering over his shoulder.

"Oh, it's just my stock portfolio," Leo replied, a touch of pride in his voice.

Grace tilted her head, her eyebrows raising with genuine curiosity. "Stock portfolio? You mean, like... money in the air?"

Leo blinked. "Not... exactly. It's money invested in companies. I watch it closely to see how it grows, or... well, in this case, dips slightly." He attempted a self-assured laugh, trying to play it cool.

Grace laughed. "So, you sit there watching imaginary numbers, hoping they get bigger?"

Leo was momentarily speechless. He had never heard his entire financial empire summarized as "imaginary numbers." "It's not quite like that. I mean, stocks reflect the real world... trends, company growth, market factors..."

Grace chuckled again. "Right. But isn't it strange to let numbers on a screen decide if you're happy or not? Seems... exhausting."

Leo was taken aback. He'd never questioned it before—watching his investments was as natural as breathing. But the way Grace put it made him realize how absurd it might sound to someone who had never lived his lifestyle.

By the late afternoon, they were both covered in dust, dirt, and—much to Leo's horror—sweat. They took a break, and Leo, though tired, felt a strange sense of satisfaction he couldn't quite place.

"So, Grace, you've been doing this for a while?" he asked, trying to learn more about this intriguing enigma.

"Yep, been volunteering here for the past few years," she replied, taking a sip of water. "I don't make much, but it's enough. I get to work with people I care about and do work that matters."

"Do you ever feel... like you're missing out on more?" Leo ventured cautiously.

Grace laughed. "More? Like... luxury cars and mansions?" She leaned back, her eyes twinkling. "Nah, not really. My life's simple, sure, but it's full of things that make me happy."

Leo couldn't help but smile. "You don't ever wonder what it's like to have... well, everything?"

She shrugged. "Honestly? Having everything sounds like a lot to handle. And from what I've seen, it doesn't necessarily make people happier." Her gaze lingered on him a second too long, a subtle jab he couldn't ignore.

As they resumed work, Leo found himself pondering her words. Having everything had always been his goal, the ultimate measure of success. But he couldn't shake the feeling that there was something he was missing—something he couldn't buy.

They continued their work in relative silence, with Grace occasionally breaking it to offer amusing commentary on the absurdities she observed in the nonprofit world. Leo found himself chuckling at her stories of eccentric patrons, including the man who donated a statue of himself to a remote school and the woman who insisted on naming every water well after her favorite pets.

The easy banter felt refreshing, and Leo realized he hadn't laughed this naturally in... well, he couldn't remember the last time.

At the end of the day, as they were finishing up, Leo noticed something unusual. Grace's face bore a serene, contented smile as she packed up her things, chatting easily with the other volunteers. She exuded a happiness that seemed foreign to Leo, like a warm light in the center of a cold room.

"Grace," he said as they were leaving, "you really seem to love this work."

She looked at him, a hint of surprise on her face. "I do. It's not about what you have, Leo. It's about what you give."

Leo frowned, feeling an uncomfortable tug in his chest. He had always believed that his happiness was linked to accumulation, to power, and to influence. But Grace was challenging everything he thought he knew. She had little, yet she seemed happier than him. How was that possible?

Seeing his bewildered expression, Grace grinned. "You look like you've seen a ghost."

Leo managed a chuckle, albeit a weak one. "It's just... surprising, I suppose. You don't have the things most people strive for, yet you seem... fulfilled."

Grace nodded thoughtfully. "Maybe it's because I don't measure my life in things. Life's too short to be constantly chasing more. Sometimes, what you need is already right in front of you."

Her words hung in the air, and for the first time in his life, Leo felt his carefully constructed beliefs start to wobble. He didn't know if he agreed with her, but he couldn't deny the tiny crack she'd managed to make.

"Leo, not everything valuable in life has a price tag. Some of the best things are unpaid," she said, smiling, and with that, she turned and walked away, leaving him standing there in quiet contemplation.

Back in his luxurious penthouse, Leo replayed the events of the day. He was surrounded by evidence of his success—artwork, rare wine, the latest tech gadgets. Yet, the memory of Grace's smile and her gentle, almost teasing wisdom lingered.

For the first time in years, he felt restless, staring out the window, watching the city's lights flicker. Leo knew his life was full of abundance, but suddenly, it seemed strangely empty.

As he lay in bed that night, unable to sleep, Leo wondered if maybe, just maybe, he'd missed something crucial along the way. And for reasons he couldn't quite explain, he found himself smiling in the dark, thinking of Grace's unpaid smile, realizing he had just experienced his first step beyond the world of profits and investments into something else—something uncharted.

Chapter 5: High Stakes, Low Impact

Leo Masters wasn't one to back down from a challenge. As much as he liked to pretend he could laugh off his friends' jabs, something about his last conversation with them had struck a nerve. Leo's childhood friends were among the few people in his life who didn't mince words with him. They were always quick to remind him that beneath the layers of wealth and luxury, he was still just Leo, a guy they'd known since the days of cheap takeaway dinners and shared rides to school.

"You're all talk, Leo," one of them had quipped over their usual poker night.

"Yeah, let's see you actually get your hands dirty," another chimed in, smirking as he tossed his cards on the table. The rest of the table had erupted in laughter.

"Alright, alright," Leo grumbled, feeling his face flush despite himself. "Fine. Name your dare, and I'll do it."

The friends exchanged a few conspiratorial glances before someone suggested, "Volunteer at the Eastwood Community Center. You know, actually lend a hand."

Leo had feigned a confident laugh, but his stomach flipped. He wasn't exactly the volunteer type. But he was in too deep to back out now.

As Leo arrived at Eastwood Community Center that Saturday morning, he immediately regretted his bravado. The building was an unassuming brick structure nestled between a laundromat and a bakery. It lacked the polished exterior he was used to, with peeling paint and a sign that looked like it had been hung back in the '90s and never touched again. He took a deep breath and walked inside, feeling conspicuously out of place in his designer jeans and spotless sneakers.

A cheery woman at the front desk greeted him. Her name tag read "Betty." She had silver hair tied back in a neat bun, with a face that seemed permanently set in a smile.

"Good morning! You must be... Leo?" she asked, squinting at the sign-up sheet on the counter.

"That's right," he replied, trying to sound at ease. "Here to... volunteer."

Betty's eyes twinkled as she handed him a neon green apron. "Fantastic! We can use all the help we can get. Today we're serving lunch to about fifty seniors, plus setting up for our after-school program."

Leo blinked. "Seniors and kids. Got it."

"Hope you're ready for some action," she said with a chuckle.

Leo managed a smile and nodded, but inside, he was completely out of his depth. He had no clue what he'd signed up for, and he suspected it would be a long day.

Leo's first task was simple: serve soup to the seniors arriving for lunch. Or so it seemed.

The kitchen was bustling, with a dozen volunteers darting back and forth, preparing trays of sandwiches and stirring massive pots of soup. The sheer volume of activity overwhelmed Leo, who usually had a personal chef to handle anything remotely food-related.

Betty handed him a ladle and gestured to a pot of minestrone. "Just fill each bowl about three-quarters of the way. Simple enough, right?"

"Easy," Leo said confidently, taking his place by the pot. He'd served countless clients deals worth millions; how hard could it be to serve a bowl of soup?

As he ladled the first bowl, he concentrated, aiming for exactly three-quarters full. But his hands, unused to this kind of manual work, trembled slightly, and the soup splashed over the edge.

"Oops," he mumbled, quickly reaching for a napkin.

One of the seniors watching nearby chuckled. "First day, kid?"

"Something like that," Leo admitted, smiling sheepishly as he dabbed at the spill.

As he served the next few bowls, he found his rhythm, but his technique left much to be desired. His ladling style was erratic, leading to an inconsistent array of soup levels that drew bemused stares from his fellow volunteers. Betty, noticing his struggle, finally came over and gently adjusted his grip.

"There you go. Nice and steady, like you're scooping up... well, maybe not millions, but something valuable," she teased, winking.

Leo smirked. "Thanks, Betty. I'm a fast learner."

But just as he'd started to get the hang of it, disaster struck. Reaching for a bowl, his ladle slipped, sending a small wave of minestrone right onto his spotless sneakers. He froze, horrified, while a few of the seniors stifled laughter.

"Looks like you've been officially baptized by the soup," one of the elderly men joked, and Leo couldn't help but laugh along.

Once the soup was served, Betty assigned him to set the tables for the after-school program. He was handed a stack of napkins and instructed to fold them "creatively" for the kids.

Now, Leo was no stranger to creativity—in business. Napkin folding, however, was an entirely different beast. He spent the next fifteen minutes experimenting with various shapes: triangles, squares, something resembling a crumpled fan. Each attempt looked worse than the last.

A group of kids, watching him from a distance, burst into laughter.

"Are they... laughing at me?" Leo asked, eyeing the kids suspiciously.

Betty stifled a chuckle of her own. "They just don't see many grown-ups struggle with napkins," she replied kindly. "Here, let me show you a trick." In seconds, she transformed one of his crumpled attempts into a neat little pouch.

Leo tried to copy her, but his fingers, accustomed to tapping keyboards and signing documents, fumbled hopelessly. Betty's eyes sparkled with amusement.

"I can do this," Leo muttered to himself, feeling a determination he usually reserved for high-stakes meetings.

Eventually, he managed to create a basic fold that didn't look too terrible. The kids seemed satisfied, which was all the encouragement he needed.

As the afternoon rolled on, Leo's initial awkwardness began to fade. He was still clumsy, but with every new task, he felt himself relaxing. He helped serve cookies, albeit after nearly dropping a whole tray. He even played a quick game of cards with one of the seniors, though he lost terribly.

During a lull, he struck up a conversation with Tom, one of the longtime volunteers.

"So, you do this every week?" Leo asked, genuinely curious.

"Yep, been coming here for fifteen years," Tom replied, arranging cups of juice on a tray. "Keeps me grounded. You meet all sorts of people, and the community here is like family."

"Don't you miss... I don't know, the excitement?" Leo asked, gesturing vaguely as though 'excitement' was some kind of currency.

Tom chuckled. "Excitement? Trust me, this place is full of it. You never know what's going to happen, and every day, you leave feeling like you made a difference."

Leo was silent, absorbing the words. There was a satisfaction here that he hadn't felt in his world of boardrooms and investments. It wasn't flashy or measurable, but it was real.

Near the end of his shift, Leo was helping to pack up the leftover supplies when Betty approached him, a smile softening her lined face.

"You did well today, Leo," she said, patting his arm. "You gave everyone a good laugh."

Leo chuckled. "I think I made more of a mess than anything else."

Betty shook her head. "Oh, no. You brought a lot of joy to people today. You don't see it, but the seniors loved watching you struggle with that soup. You made them laugh—some of them hadn't smiled like that in ages."

Leo was quiet, taken aback. He'd always been celebrated for his business acumen, his ability to turn a profit, his sharp instincts. But here, in this simple community center, he was appreciated for... well, bumbling attempts and good humor.

It felt strange and humbling.

As he said his goodbyes and left the community center, Leo felt a sense of warmth he couldn't explain. He'd faced plenty of high-stakes moments in his life, but nothing quite like this. The "low-impact" tasks of folding napkins, serving soup, and chatting with the seniors had brought him a kind of joy he hadn't expected.

Climbing into his car, he felt lighter, more at ease. He chuckled, imagining his friends' faces when he told them about his day. And he knew he'd be back at Eastwood, even if just to give the seniors another laugh.

For the first time in a long time, Leo felt that maybe his worth wasn't in the numbers he raked in, but in the small moments, the shared laughter, and the lives he touched—even if only in the tiniest ways.

As he pulled away, he realized he couldn't wait to share the story with Grace, hoping she'd find his bumbling attempts as funny as everyone else did. And perhaps, in his own clumsy way, he was inching closer to a life of real impact, one small, humble task at a time.

Chapter 6: The Tax Write-Off

Leo Masters wasn't someone who made hasty financial decisions—at least, not without some benefit. His world ran on margins, spreadsheets, and meticulously calculated risks. So, when he began considering a donation to the Eastwood Community Center, he naturally framed it as a "tax write-off." After all, his accountants had been badgering him to explore "charitable options" to balance his corporate deductions. It wasn't like him to turn down a good tax benefit, and if it also happened to improve his public image? All the better.

As he ran the numbers that morning, Leo couldn't help feeling a sense of pride at his so-called "altruism." A healthy donation would cover his tax benefit for the quarter and spare him another tongue-lashing from his PR consultant, who had been hounding him to soften his "calculating" reputation. A donation to a local community center felt like an easy win-win, allowing him to brush off any lingering sentimental ties while still looking like the good guy.

His fingers hovered over the checkbook, debating how much felt "generous yet strategic." Ten thousand dollars? That seemed like a safe number—not so much that it would raise eyebrows among his shareholders, but still enough to impress the center's modest staff. With a pleased grin, he scribbled his signature at the bottom, his penmanship curiously flawless in his excitement.

It was only after he'd sealed the envelope and finished mentally calculating his post-deduction gains that a faint, nagging thought entered his mind: What if, just once, he made a donation without expecting anything back?

He quickly brushed the notion aside. No need to get carried away. This was still business, after all.

Later that afternoon, Leo arrived at Eastwood, his donation check tucked safely in his jacket pocket. He'd decided to deliver it in person, if only to soak up the gratitude that he knew would follow. After his awkward but surprisingly enjoyable day volunteering last week, he felt oddly drawn to the place. He had mentally framed the visit as a final wrap-up—one more moment of positive PR, and he'd be on his way.

As he walked through the center's doors, he was greeted by Betty, who flashed him her trademark smile. "Leo! Back so soon? I thought we might have scared you off."

Leo chuckled, adjusting his collar. "You nearly did," he replied with a grin. "But, I figured it was worth another trip."

Betty's eyes twinkled as she led him down the hall. "Well, we're happy to have you. The seniors are still talking about your soup-serving skills."

Leo raised his eyebrows, managing a laugh. "If that's what you call 'skills.' But, actually, I came by today to drop off a donation."

The words felt strange on his tongue, and he watched Betty's face carefully, looking for the reaction he was used to: awe, surprise, maybe even a little disbelief. But instead, her expression softened with a gentle smile.

"Oh, Leo, that's wonderful. Thank you," she said warmly. "Every bit goes a long way here."

Something about the simplicity of her response caught him off-guard. There was no over-the-top reaction, no desperate gratitude. Just an honest, heartfelt thanks that left him momentarily speechless.

As Betty led Leo into the main room, he noticed a small group of community members gathered around tables, chatting and laughing. Betty announced his donation with minimal fanfare, and there was a round of applause that sounded almost absurdly genuine. People looked at him with a warmth and sincerity he hadn't quite encountered before.

One of the seniors from last week, Mr. Henderson, called out, "Thanks, young man! Guess that soup disaster didn't scare you off after all."

Laughter erupted around the room, and Leo felt his face flush. "Well, I figured a check might make up for the... soup incidents," he replied, scratching the back of his head.

A woman in her late forties approached him, holding the hand of a young girl who looked about seven. "Mr. Masters," she said softly, "I'm Sarah, and this is my daughter, Lily. I wanted to thank you for helping the center. It means so much to families like ours."

Leo managed a polite nod, feeling awkward. He had been thanked countless times for investments, for creating jobs, and for making profits. But this gratitude was different. It wasn't laced with professional expectations or opportunistic ambitions. It was raw and sincere.

As he knelt to greet Lily, she handed him a small, colorful drawing of the community center. "Thank you for helping us," she whispered shyly, her cheeks reddening.

Leo took the drawing, his heart feeling strangely heavy. "You're very welcome, Lily," he replied, managing a soft smile. "It's... nice to be here."

As he mingled with the members of Eastwood, Leo's internal dialogue became a chaotic scramble to justify his actions as purely "business." He reminded himself about the tax write-off, the PR value, and the intangible gains. Yet, as he looked around, he found it harder to keep the mask in place. Each thank-you, each small gesture of appreciation, chipped away at his carefully constructed façade.

"Come on, Masters," he muttered under his breath. "It's just a check. Nothing revolutionary here."

But every time he repeated this, the conviction weakened. Each interaction—each smile and grateful gaze—seemed to undermine his usual justifications.

While lost in his thoughts, he spotted a familiar face by the doorway—Grace, the volunteer he'd met last week, who had sparked his initial curiosity about life outside his bubble. She waved, her face lighting up with the same sincere joy that had intrigued him so deeply.

"Leo! Good to see you back!" she called out, approaching him with an enthusiastic smile. "I didn't think you'd come back after the soup incident."

He laughed, grateful for her lighthearted teasing. "I figured I'd redeem myself with a donation. You know, start fresh."

Grace's eyes softened. "It's very generous of you. The center does so much for the community, and this donation will help a lot of people."

Leo couldn't help but notice the difference in her tone. It wasn't the usual praise he received. Grace's appreciation was deeper, more personal, as if she knew exactly how much impact that money would have.

He glanced away, scratching his chin awkwardly. "It's... nothing really. Just a little write-off, you know?"

Grace gave him a look that was both amused and a little sad. "Well whatever your reason, it means the world to us. I just hope someday you'll see it that way too."

Her words lingered in his mind, making him uncomfortable. He wasn't used to being questioned about his motives. Yet, instead of feeling defensive, he felt... challenged.

As the day wound down, Betty approached Leo with a curious gleam in her eye. "Leo," she began, "we usually have a little thank-you gathering for our larger donors, just a small way to show our appreciation. It'd be wonderful if you could join us next week for a casual dinner here."

Leo hesitated, feeling a pang of discomfort. A thank-you dinner? He wasn't sure he deserved—or wanted—that level of appreciation. But before he could protest, Betty patted his arm with a smile and said, "We'll see you there. It'll be good fun."

He tried to argue, but she'd already moved off, leaving him cornered into an invitation he couldn't refuse.

On the drive home, Leo's mind was a whirlwind of emotions. The applause, the handshakes, the heartfelt thanks—none of it felt like the predictable rewards he was used to. These people weren't angling for business connections or hoping to secure investments. They were simply thankful for the gesture itself, expecting nothing in return.

As he flipped the car stereo on, trying to shake off the unfamiliar feelings, he realized with a start that he felt... satisfied. Not the usual satisfaction of a successful deal, but something softer, warmer. It was a strange feeling, uncomfortable but not unpleasant.

"Come on, Masters," he muttered to himself. "It's a tax write-off, plain and simple."

But his reflection in the rear-view mirror told a different story. There was something in his eyes, a vulnerability he didn't recognize. For once, the "bottom line" didn't seem to matter.

Over the next few days, Leo found himself daydreaming about Eastwood, its volunteers, and the odd feeling of contentment he'd felt there. He began researching community initiatives and charities, something he had never felt compelled to do before. At first, he told himself it was purely for tax purposes, but the excitement building inside him told a different story.

And, of course, he kept replaying his conversation with Grace. Her words echoed in his mind, nudging him to consider whether he could ever truly give without expecting something in return.

After his research, he realized he had been wrong about community centers like Eastwood. They weren't just places where people went for help; they were places where people found purpose, where lives changed in the smallest but most impactful ways.

He couldn't shake the nagging feeling that maybe, just maybe, he'd been missing out on something all these years.

By the time the thank-you dinner approached, Leo was almost eager to return to Eastwood. He told himself it was out of courtesy, that he was merely responding to Betty's invitation. But deep down, he knew there was more to it. He wanted to be there, to feel that unfiltered appreciation again, to experience that sense of belonging he had rarely encountered.

And so, with an open mind and a heart that, for the first time, wasn't focused on the bottom line, Leo made his way back to Eastwood, wondering just how much he might have yet to learn about giving—and perhaps about himself.

Chapter 7: The Money Can't Fix Everything Moment

Leo Masters was used to a life where problems had price tags. And if there was one thing he never lacked, it was money. When issues arose, he could always solve them with a well-placed call, an expensive consultant, or a bit of flashy spending. But nothing had prepared him for the curveball life threw his way when he received a panicked call from his old family friend, Aunt Millie.

Aunt Millie wasn't his actual aunt but had been a close friend of his parents ever since Leo could remember. She'd been around for birthday parties, his high school graduation, and every family Christmas, usually bearing homemade cookies and unsolicited life advice. To her, Leo was still the mischievous kid with too much energy and not enough sense. So, when she called him in a panic, he didn't hesitate to offer his help, assuming it would be a straightforward fix.

"Leo, it's about Alex," Aunt Millie said, her voice thick with worry. Alex was her only child, a kid Leo had practically grown up with. "He's been acting strange lately, not himself. I'm really worried."

Leo felt an automatic response rise in his throat: "What do you need? Money? I could set him up with a high-end therapist or... I don't know, maybe get him a new car to cheer him up?"

"No, Leo," Aunt Millie sighed, "It's not about money. I think he's going through something. He won't talk to me, and I just don't know what to do anymore. I thought maybe he'd talk to you."

Leo hesitated, caught off guard. He had no idea how to help someone talk about their feelings. But seeing as Aunt Millie was practically family, he couldn't just brush it off.

"Alright, I'll see what I can do," he said reluctantly, picturing himself breezing in, handing Alex a wad of cash, and calling it a day. He had no idea what lay ahead.

Leo showed up at Aunt Millie's house later that evening, wearing a blazer that screamed "business mogul" far more than "concerned friend." He found Alex in the garage, tinkering with an old motorcycle. The space was cluttered with tools, oil-stained rags, and half-finished projects that looked entirely foreign to Leo.

"Hey, Alex!" Leo called out with what he hoped was a casual wave.

Alex looked up, clearly surprised. "Leo? What are you doing here?"

"Oh, you know," Leo said, trying to sound nonchalant. "Just thought I'd stop by, check on things. See how you're doing."

Alex raised an eyebrow. "Alright. Well... I'm fine."

Leo cleared his throat. "Listen, if you're having a tough time, you know, with... whatever, I'm here. I mean, if there's anything I can buy—uh, I mean, do—to help, just let me know."

Alex smirked, setting down his wrench. "I don't think you can 'buy' your way out of this one, Leo."

Leo blinked, thrown by the remark. "Oh, come on. I could get you a new bike, a therapist, or maybe just book you a trip to Europe? Clear your mind and all that."

Alex shook his head, laughing. "Leo, I'm not even sure you understand what's going on. I'm not... it's not something you can fix with money."

The next day, Leo, convinced he just needed to approach Alex's situation from a new angle, came up with a list of elaborate solutions to "cheer him up." First on his list: a brand-new gaming setup.

Leo showed up at Alex's garage once again, this time with a box filled with the latest tech: a high-end VR headset, a top-of-the-line gaming console, and an array of games that covered everything from action-packed shooters to relaxing simulations.

Alex looked at the setup, clearly amused. "Wow, Leo. You really went all out, huh?"

A HEART'S INVESTMENT - BEYOND BILLIONS

Leo grinned, feeling confident. "Yep! I figured some high-quality gaming might take your mind off things. You know, get you out of the funk or whatever."

Alex looked at the VR headset, a slight smirk forming. "You think I'm just stressed out and need to 'game' my worries away?"

"Why not?" Leo shrugged. "It works for a lot of people."

Alex shook his head, still smiling but with a tinge of sadness in his eyes. "Thanks, Leo. I appreciate it, but this isn't going to solve anything."

Leo was baffled. He'd been certain that a shiny new gadget would do the trick. He was at a loss as he realized this problem might actually be beyond his usual skill set of throwing money at it.

Frustrated, Leo found himself in Aunt Millie's kitchen that evening, sipping herbal tea and desperately hoping she could offer some insight. She watched him carefully, a knowing glint in her eye.

"Leo, you're not used to this, are you?" she asked, a small smile playing on her lips.

"Used to what? I offered him everything I could think of. A new bike, a European vacation, even a full gaming setup. He didn't want any of it," Leo huffed, genuinely confused.

Aunt Millie chuckled, reaching over to pat his hand. "Oh, Leo. Some things can't be bought. Alex doesn't need material things; he needs someone who actually understands him."

Leo frowned. "But I'm not... well, I'm not exactly equipped for deep talks and emotional stuff. I thought a solid distraction would do the trick."

"That's the problem," Aunt Millie replied gently. "You can't distract him from his feelings. He needs to process them, and sometimes, all he needs is someone to listen."

Taking Aunt Millie's words to heart, Leo decided to take a different approach. The next day, he returned to the garage, this time empty-handed.

"Alright, Alex," he said, sitting on an old chair and folding his hands in his lap. "I'm here to... listen."

Alex snorted. "Listen, huh? You, the guy who checks his phone every three seconds?"

Leo shifted uncomfortably, forcing himself to keep his phone in his pocket. "I'm serious, Alex. Tell me what's going on."

After a long pause, Alex sighed. "It's just... life, you know? I feel like I'm going nowhere. My friends are getting ahead, starting careers, and I'm stuck here, fixing old bikes and barely scraping by."

Leo nodded, trying to appear wise. "I see... I mean, I can offer you a job if you want? Or maybe, I could fund a startup for you—something to give you a kick-start?"

Alex chuckled, rolling his eyes. "Leo, this isn't about money. It's about purpose. I feel like I don't have a direction, like I'm just... floating."

Leo scratched his head, feeling genuinely puzzled. Purpose? Direction? These weren't things you could pick up at a store. But he tried to stay focused, pushing through the urge to suggest yet another financial solution.

As days passed, Leo continued to wrestle with his growing helplessness. Nothing in his wealth or power seemed to make a difference in helping Alex find his footing. It gnawed at him, challenging everything he believed about control and influence.

One afternoon, he ran into Grace at Eastwood while attending a community event he'd been invited to after his donation. He recounted his ongoing struggles with Alex, almost in a daze.

Grace listened quietly, her eyes kind but amused. "Leo, you're fighting against a wall here. Money is amazing for certain things, but it's a terrible substitute for meaning. Alex needs someone who actually cares about him and his life. Sometimes, that's enough."

Her words hit him like a punch. Money wasn't the solution here; it was presence, empathy, and actual human connection.

Armed with Grace's advice, Leo approached Alex one more time. This time, he wasn't there to fix anything. He was there to share something real, something he rarely showed anyone: vulnerability.

"You know, Alex," he began, struggling to find the right words, "I don't have all the answers either. I've been lucky enough to make money, sure, but I've got my own issues. It's not like I can buy purpose. If I could, I'd probably be a happier guy."

Alex looked at him, genuinely surprised. "Really? I thought you had everything figured out."

Leo laughed bitterly. "Not even close. But I think that's okay. Maybe we're both just... figuring things out."

For the first time, Leo saw a flicker of understanding in Alex's eyes. It was the first time he'd connected with someone over something deeper than business or assets.

As Leo left that evening, he felt a weight lift from his shoulders. He hadn't solved Alex's problems, but he'd shown up and listened. And for once, that felt like enough. He was beginning to see the world differently—not as a series of investments but as a web of relationships, where empathy and presence held more value than he'd ever realized.

The experience left him questioning his own life choices, his relentless focus on success and money. Perhaps, he thought, true wealth wasn't about the bank balance but the lives he could touch.

And as he drove home that night, Leo knew that the version of himself who entered Aunt Millie's house just a week ago was already changing, slowly but surely.

Chapter 8: The Unmarketable Smile

Leo Masters was no stranger to metrics, margins, and ROI calculations, yet when it came to understanding happiness, he was as lost as a penguin in a desert. So, when he found himself intrigued by Grace's seemingly boundless joy in everyday moments, he was determined to analyze it in his own peculiar, business-minded way.

It had been a few weeks since he'd first met her, and her genuine delight in the simplest of things baffled him. Her job at Eastwood Community Center paid peanuts by his standards. Yet, she seemed as thrilled about life as if she were worth billions. Curiosity—and maybe a pinch of something else he couldn't quite name—drew him back to Eastwood to see her again.

Leo approached Grace's corner of the community center, where she was chatting animatedly with a group of elderly residents, her laughter echoing through the room. She was holding up a poorly knitted scarf, looped in haphazard colors, and clapping her hands with genuine enthusiasm as a beaming elderly woman claimed it was her "masterpiece."

"Not too shabby, Edna!" Grace chirped, grinning from ear to ear.

Leo observed, tilting his head in mild disbelief. *Is this... profitable?* he wondered, squinting slightly as if he could somehow see the invisible profit margin in the air.

Eventually, Grace noticed him standing there. She waved him over, her smile as bright as ever.

"Leo! What brings you back here?" she asked, sounding pleasantly surprised.

"Oh, you know... just... observing," he replied awkwardly, shoving his hands into his pockets.

Grace raised an eyebrow, clearly amused. "Observing what exactly?"

Leo cleared his throat. "You know, just... watching how you, uh, operate. I mean, the way you seem so happy doing... all this," he gestured vaguely to the room of elderly folks and craft supplies. "Don't you ever think about doing something more, I don't know, lucrative?"

Grace laughed, the sound light and genuine. "Leo, if I were measuring my life by dollar signs, I'd be the world's poorest person. I prefer other ways to measure wealth."

Leo blinked, feeling like he'd just heard something in a foreign language. "Other ways to measure wealth?"

Grace nodded, her smile warm. "Yep. Happiness, satisfaction, a sense of purpose—things you can't exactly quantify."

Leo stared at her, perplexed. "You're telling me you don't measure your happiness by your paycheck?"

Grace laughed again, shaking her head. "Nope! In fact, I think it's pretty freeing not to have that hanging over my head. It lets me focus on things that actually matter to me."

Leo scratched his head, struggling to comprehend. *So... intangible assets? Is that what she's talking about?*

Determined to figure this out, Leo decided to spend the afternoon shadowing Grace. She introduced him to various "clients"—elderly folks with twinkling eyes, middle-aged volunteers with unglamorous but warm smiles, and children who dashed through the room with wild giggles. Each interaction left him more bewildered.

At one point, Grace led him to a small garden behind the community center. Together, they knelt in the soil, pulling weeds and planting flowers.

"So," he began, looking down at his dirt-caked hands, "you find this... enjoyable?"

Grace grinned, wiping sweat from her brow. "Yep! There's something satisfying about nurturing things. Besides, it's grounding."

Leo narrowed his eyes. "Grounding? Like, grounding an investment?"

Grace laughed so hard she nearly fell into the flower bed. "No, Leo! Like connecting with nature. It's peaceful. There's no market price, no quarterly report... just me, the plants, and a little dirt."

He tried to process this, feeling like a computer that had just received incompatible software. *No market price? No ROI?* He squinted at the plants as if hoping they'd suddenly sprout dollar signs. But nothing happened.

Throughout the afternoon, Leo caught glimpses of Grace's smile. It wasn't the polite kind he'd seen at business functions or the forced type he'd plaster on his face when shaking hands with investors. This was something else entirely. It was genuine, unguarded, and completely unaffected.

"Grace," he blurted out at one point, "how do you do it?"

"Do what?" she asked, brushing a bit of soil off her hand.

"Be so... content with so little."

Grace's eyes softened. "I wouldn't say I have 'little,' Leo. I have relationships, a purpose, a community. Those are the things that fill me up."

Leo paused, staring down at the plants again. "But what about security? Don't you ever worry about... you know, not having enough?"

Grace shrugged. "Security's nice, but what's the point if it costs you happiness? Money isn't the only way to feel secure. I have friends, family, and a community that looks out for me. That's a kind of security you can't put a price on."

Leo mulled this over, scratching his head. "So, in your, uh... ledger of life, it's all about connections?"

Grace grinned. "Exactly! In the end, it's about people, not profits. When you have that, you'll find you're pretty rich—even if you're not a billionaire."

Trying to put his theory into practice, Leo resolved to do something meaningful—or as meaningful as he could manage. He returned to the community center the next day with a gift: a box of artisanal chocolates he'd bought from a high-end shop in town.

"Here," he said, handing them to Grace with an awkward smile. "For you. Just... as a thank you."

Grace chuckled, accepting the box. "Thank you, Leo. But you know, you didn't have to bring me anything."

Leo scratched his head. "Yeah, but I wanted to... you know, show appreciation. I guess."

Grace nodded, popping open the box and offering him a chocolate. "You're starting to get it. Appreciation doesn't always come with a price tag, though. Sometimes, just being here is enough."

Leo bit into a chocolate, mulling over her words. It was absurd, really, how foreign the concept was to him. He'd always considered appreciation to be a transaction—a bonus, a gift, a grand gesture. But to Grace, it was as simple as showing up.

Later that week, Leo found himself volunteering again, this time at a fundraising event for the community center. Grace was running the event, which was held in a local park and featured various booths, games, and food stalls. Leo manned the ticket booth—a job that required more patience than he thought he possessed. For hours, he exchanged dollar bills for tickets, watching families laugh, kids run around, and neighbors greet each other.

At one point, Grace approached him, holding a bundle of raffle tickets. "Having fun?" she asked, a mischievous glint in her eye.

Leo shrugged, his face splitting into a reluctant smile. "Surprisingly, yeah. I mean, there's no ROI on this, no fancy spreadsheets... but somehow, it feels... good?"

Grace beamed. "See? Some things can't be measured, Leo. But they're still valuable."

He stared at her, watching as she handed raffle tickets to a group of kids who lit up with excitement. That smile—her smile—felt as if it could light up a whole city. And it had nothing to do with wealth, power, or influence.

Over the following weeks, Leo found himself increasingly drawn to the community center. Every visit left him feeling lighter, as if he was seeing the world through a new lens. He began to notice things he'd previously overlooked: the warmth in people's laughter, the quiet contentment of shared silence, and the genuine appreciation for simple moments.

One day, as he sat with Grace in the park after an event, he looked at her with newfound understanding. "You know, I think I finally get it. All these things I used to overlook... they're actually worth something."

Grace nodded, smiling. "Exactly. Wealth isn't always about what you have, but about what you give. And sometimes, the biggest impact comes from the smallest gestures."

Leo's usual response would have been a retort about the tangible benefits of tangible assets, but he just smiled. He realized, sitting there in the park, that he was richer in that moment than he'd ever felt in his life. And it wasn't because of his bank account.

As they watched the sun set over the park, he felt a strange sense of contentment settle over him—a warmth that wasn't bought, brokered, or traded. It was just... there.

And for the first time in a long while, Leo Masters was at peace.

Chapter 9: The Currency of Kindness

Leo Masters had always understood currency in cold, calculable terms: dollars, stocks, assets. Kindness, on the other hand, was a resource he'd never bothered to invest in—until now. Inspired by Grace's seemingly boundless goodwill and the inexplicable satisfaction he'd felt volunteering, he decided he'd attempt his own "acts of kindness."

In his mind, kindness had to be strategic. After all, every asset he'd acquired had come from a well-planned move. Why should goodwill be any different?

Leo's first attempt at spreading kindness was bold and—characteristically—over the top. He kicked things off by heading to his high-rise office, where he saw his usual gaggle of assistants, administrative staff, and security. Determined to make an impression, he cleared his throat and addressed the room.

"Everyone," he announced, "I just want to say how much I... appreciate... all of you."

His words landed awkwardly. His assistant, Cynthia, looked up from her laptop with a raised eyebrow. "Is everything alright, sir?" she asked cautiously.

"Yes, Cynthia, absolutely," he said, frowning as he fumbled for the right words. "I was just, you know, thinking about kindness. And I want you all to know... your work here is valued."

His team exchanged confused glances. Sensing he hadn't quite conveyed the warmth he'd intended, Leo cleared his throat again and went for broke.

"To show my appreciation," he continued with a flourish, "I'm treating everyone to... lunch! At the deli downstairs!"

A few staff members looked at each other, stifling smiles. "That's very thoughtful, sir," Cynthia said, struggling to hide her amusement.

Leo didn't miss the note of pity in her voice. *Was I too generous?* he wondered.

Still, he trudged down to the deli himself, determined to see the plan through. Leo, who'd never ordered his own lunch before, ended up buying sandwiches for the whole office. But when he handed them out, the sight of his employees politely thanking him with faint amusement was underwhelming. *Was kindness supposed to feel... more exhilarating?* he thought, frowning as he munched on his own tasteless turkey club.

Leo knew he had to aim higher. Remembering a story he'd heard about a man who'd gone viral for paying for strangers' groceries, he decided to replicate this "act of kindness."

Dressed in his usual sharp suit, Leo strolled down to a bustling grocery store and loitered by the checkout lanes, scanning the shoppers. Finally, he spotted an elderly woman in a faded cardigan, her cart filled with canned beans, pasta, and a suspiciously large number of cat food cans. Perfect.

With a confident stride, he approached her. "Excuse me, ma'am," he said, in what he hoped was a soothing voice, "I'd like to pay for your groceries."

The woman squinted at him, clearly baffled. "Why would you want to do that?" she asked suspiciously.

"Uh, well... as an act of kindness?" Leo offered, unsure why she looked so bewildered. "I thought it might brighten your day."

Her eyes narrowed. "What's the catch?"

Leo blinked. "No catch! Just... kindness."

She eyed him for a moment longer before shrugging. "Alright, if you insist."

Leo pulled out his credit card, grinning as he swiped it with a flourish, anticipating her heartfelt gratitude. But instead, she gave him a curt nod and mumbled, "Thanks, sonny," before trundling away, muttering something about "weird rich folks."

Leo stood there, his card still in his hand, feeling slightly deflated. *Maybe kindness isn't just about paying for things,* he mused. *Maybe there's more to it.*

Still determined, Leo returned to the community center, hoping that another round of volunteering might offer some answers. He arrived in the middle of lunch service, where Grace was overseeing a bustling group of volunteers ladling soup, handing out bread, and chatting with the patrons.

Leo sidled up to her, trying to look casual. "Need an extra pair of hands?"

Grace raised an amused eyebrow. "You volunteering? Again?"

He nodded, feeling slightly self-conscious. "Yes, I'm... trying something new. You know, spreading kindness."

Grace chuckled, handing him a ladle. "Alright, Mr. Kindness. You're on soup duty."

With a deep breath, Leo took his position behind the table, spooning ladles of soup into bowls with what he hoped was an air of genuine warmth. He attempted to chat with the patrons, asking how their day was or offering an awkward "enjoy your meal," but his attempts felt forced.

As he served one elderly man a bowl of soup, the man eyed him with a twinkle in his eye. "You're new, aren't ya? Usually, the young ones smile more."

Leo, taken aback, forced a tight smile. "Right. Smiling. Of course."

The man chuckled and shuffled off, leaving Leo feeling like he'd been given a C-minus on his "kindness report card."

It was at this point, as Leo was feeling increasingly uncertain about his "kindness strategy," that he spotted Grace speaking to a small girl with curly hair and a shy smile. Grace crouched down, holding the girl's hands as they chatted, and soon, the girl's face lit up with a broad grin. Leo couldn't hear what they were saying, but he could see the genuine joy on the girl's face—and Grace's, too.

Maybe kindness isn't about grand gestures, he realized. *Maybe it's just... showing up.*

As he pondered this, a patron called out to him. "Hey, soup guy! Got any bread?"

Leo snapped out of his thoughts, quickly grabbing a bread roll. But this time, he didn't just hand it over. He looked the man in the eye, smiled, and said, "Enjoy."

The man grinned back, nodding. "Thanks, pal."

And just like that, Leo felt a small spark of warmth he hadn't anticipated.

After lunch service, Leo sat down beside Grace, feeling surprisingly content. "You make this look easy," he admitted.

Grace chuckled, handing him a glass of water. "Kindness isn't a competition, Leo. It's about connection."

Leo sipped his water, nodding thoughtfully. "It's weird, though. I always thought... well, that kindness was like any other resource—you give some away, and then you have less. But the more I try, the more I feel like I have more to give."

Grace smiled, her eyes softening. "That's the beauty of it. Kindness is the only currency that grows when you share it."

He let her words sink in. All his life, he'd measured success by profits and assets. But here, at this community center, he was beginning to grasp that value wasn't always about material wealth.

Encouraged by this realization, Leo found himself approaching kindness with more authenticity and less calculation. It wasn't easy, and he often stumbled. There was the time he tried to help a young mother carry her groceries, only to accidentally drop her eggs, which splattered on the sidewalk. Then there was his attempt to give a heartfelt compliment to Cynthia, his assistant, who thought he was giving her a "performance review" and spent the next hour frantically revising her work.

But even in his blunders, Leo felt something shifting. He wasn't being kind to impress anyone or to feel powerful. He was simply... being kind.

One evening, he received a call from a community center volunteer, asking if he could pick up some supplies. Without thinking twice, he agreed. As he carried the boxes into the center, he spotted a group of kids setting up decorations for a party. They looked over at him, wide-eyed.

"Are you the one bringing the food?" one of the kids asked.

Leo grinned. "You bet."

The kids cheered, and Leo felt an unexpected warmth wash over him. He realized that these small acts—helping out, showing up, sharing his time—were enriching him in a way he'd never experienced.

At the end of the week, Grace invited him to a volunteer appreciation dinner at the community center. As they sat together, eating homemade pasta and sharing stories, Leo found himself laughing more than he had in years. The room was filled with warmth, laughter, and connection—all things he'd once considered secondary.

As the evening drew to a close, Leo found himself standing beside Grace, looking out at the bustling room. "You know, I think I finally understand what you were trying to teach me," he said quietly.

Grace looked up at him, smiling. "Oh? And what's that?"

He paused, glancing around at the volunteers and community members laughing and chatting. "Kindness... it's not something you spend. It's something that grows. It's like... an investment with infinite returns."

Grace chuckled, nudging him. "Look at you, using finance talk to explain kindness. I'm impressed."

Leo grinned. "Hey, it's what I know. But... it makes sense, right? The more you give, the more you have."

Grace nodded, her smile soft. "Exactly. And sometimes, the best returns aren't the ones you can count."

As Leo left the community center that night, he felt lighter. He no longer saw kindness as an obligation or a strategy. It had become a part of him, woven into his life not as a tool for success but as a source of joy.

The next morning, he walked into his office with a new perspective. He greeted his employees with genuine warmth, even surprising Cynthia by offering to bring her a coffee—a gesture that, to her shock, was completely sincere.

And for the first time in his life, Leo felt like he was truly rich—not in assets, but in something far more valuable. In kindness.

Chapter 10: The Lost Profit

For a man like Leo Masters, profit had always been the barometer of success. Calculations, margins, projections—these were his life's compass. But now, with his newfound appreciation for kindness, he found himself steering in uncharted waters. No spreadsheets could measure what he'd been experiencing. And for the first time in years, Leo was about to make an investment that went beyond dollars and cents. He was investing in people.

But, as it turned out, this journey wasn't nearly as straightforward as Leo had expected.

It all began with an opportunity he noticed during one of his days volunteering at the community center. The director, a well-meaning yet clearly exhausted man named Frank, mentioned in passing that they were short on funds to renovate the center's outdated facilities. The building, originally a schoolhouse, was nearing a hundred years old, and the plumbing and electrical systems were relics from another era. They were holding bake sales, car washes, and raffles, but the scale of the renovation needed was beyond their small team's reach.

Leo, overhearing this, felt an odd tug in his chest. He'd already seen firsthand how much the community center meant to people. He thought back to the smiles, the gratitude, and the sense of belonging he'd witnessed. And before he could stop himself, he found himself volunteering to make an anonymous donation—a sizable one, large enough to kickstart the renovation.

The board of the center was overjoyed. Plans were quickly drawn up, contractors consulted, and Leo felt something he hadn't felt in years: anticipation, not for a return, but simply to see this idea come to life.

Of course, the doubts began creeping in almost immediately.

The morning after he'd made the donation, Leo found himself sitting at his dining table, anxiously tapping his fingers. With a frown, he opened his laptop and began calculating exactly how much he'd pledged. The number looked far more substantial than it had the day before.

Did I go overboard? he wondered. He'd been cautious with his finances for so long that parting with this much money, especially without any expectation of financial return, felt... reckless.

To make matters worse, the renovations got off to a rocky start. Contractors missed deadlines, materials were delayed, and the cost began to inch higher with each hiccup. With each new expense report, Leo's stomach tightened. Despite his promise of anonymity, Frank would periodically send him updates to keep him in the loop.

"Minor setback," Frank wrote in one email. "Turns out the wiring needs a full replacement. But don't worry, we'll keep it as affordable as possible!"

Minor setback? Leo could practically feel the money slipping through his fingers. He knew he couldn't back out now, but he wasn't sure if his nerves could handle much more.

Leo decided he needed a way to track his "return on kindness"—a new term he'd coined to quantify what he was feeling. Surely there had to be a way to measure this investment.

He opened a blank spreadsheet, feeling a wave of comfort wash over him. If kindness had a return, he'd be able to find it here.

In Column A, he listed the various community center improvements: plumbing, electrical work, new paint, updated furniture. In Column B, he labeled it "Costs." In Column C, he hesitated, eventually labeling it "Projected Returns." He left that column blank, uncertain what he would enter.

He started adding up the numbers. The plumbing would cost nearly 20% more than originally estimated. The electrical work alone was eating up half of his contribution. As he tallied the figures, he tried to assign some form of "projected return" value to each line.

"How do you calculate the ROI on a new water heater?" he muttered to himself, rubbing his temples. After a while, he finally came up with something: "Improved morale." He entered a hypothetical value next to it, but it still didn't add up in his mind.

He even considered, in a moment of mild panic, backing out of the donation. He rationalized that he could limit his losses and perhaps still make a difference by donating time instead of money. But every time he thought of pulling out, he remembered the people he'd helped, the smiles and the handshakes, and the kids who played happily in that rundown gym. The idea of disappointing them... well, that wasn't something he wanted to deal with.

A month passed, and the expenses continued piling up. One day, Leo decided to drop by the center unannounced. He was prepared to see progress—an updated facility, maybe new paint, perhaps even a few of those new tables he'd heard about. But as he walked in, he saw... chaos.

The gym was closed off, the floors littered with paint cans, tools, and torn-up wood. Frank was pacing, talking on the phone with a contractor, looking frazzled. Leo felt his hopes deflate as he surveyed the mess.

"What... happened?" Leo asked, though he could already tell the answer wouldn't be pleasant.

Frank sighed, hanging up the phone. "It's been... rough. Turns out, the structure's weaker than we thought. Costs went up again."

Leo stared at him. "So, it's... it's not finished?"

"Not yet," Frank admitted, rubbing his forehead. "But we're doing our best. Just taking a bit longer than we'd hoped."

Leo's frustration surged. He'd poured money into this place. He'd imagined a grand reveal, a bright, newly renovated center for the community to enjoy. And here it was—a construction zone with seemingly no end in sight.

As he drove home that evening, Leo couldn't shake the feeling that he'd been too idealistic, too naive. *What was I thinking? That I could throw some money at a problem and solve it instantly?*

That evening, Leo was tempted to open up his "return on kindness" spreadsheet and type in "ZERO" under the "Projected Returns" column. But something stopped him. He thought about the kids who'd be playing basketball in that gym, the families who relied on the center for gatherings and celebrations, the volunteers who found purpose there.

He realized that his obsession with returns was clouding his perspective. Not every investment showed immediate results. And maybe that was okay.

With a sigh, Leo closed his laptop, vowing to check in on the project in a few weeks. In the meantime, he decided he'd stop by and help wherever he could, trusting that even if he couldn't see the results right now, his investment would pay off in other ways.

Several weeks later, Leo returned to the community center, bracing himself for more chaos. To his surprise, though, things looked... different. The walls were freshly painted in cheerful colors, the gym was open with brand-new flooring, and families were bustling about, enjoying the space.

Frank spotted him from across the room and hurried over, his face lit with gratitude. "Leo! You made it!"

Leo raised his eyebrows. "This is... all finished?"

Frank grinned, nodding. "We worked double-time to get it done. Wanted to surprise you."

As they walked through the center together, Frank introduced him to various families who'd benefited from the renovation. They shook his hand, thanked him, and shared how much the new facilities meant to them. Leo felt a warmth in his chest that no spreadsheet could quantify.

One young boy, holding a basketball, looked up at Leo with wide eyes. "Are you the guy who fixed the gym?"

Leo chuckled, bending down to his level. "I guess I am."

The boy grinned. "Thanks! Now we can play without tripping over stuff."

Leo laughed, ruffling the boy's hair. "You're welcome, buddy."

As he walked back to his car that evening, Leo felt lighter than he had in years. He thought back to his spreadsheet, to all the calculations he'd made, and how utterly irrelevant they felt now. There was no formula for the feeling he had, no ROI he could assign to the smiles he'd seen.

The center wasn't just a building. It was a place for connection, for community. And while the investment hadn't "paid off" in the traditional sense, it had given him something far more valuable.

For the first time in his life, Leo understood that real wealth wasn't measured in dollars, stocks, or assets. Real wealth was about impact—the kind that left a lasting mark on people's lives.

And that, he realized with a grin, was worth more than any profit he'd ever made.

Driving home, Leo felt a surge of clarity. Maybe he'd never know the full impact of his donation, and maybe the returns would always be intangible. But that was okay. For once, he didn't need an exact figure. He didn't need a net gain.

As he pulled into his driveway, Leo made a decision. His journey with kindness wasn't over. He wanted to keep investing—not just in the community center, but in people, in relationships, in moments of genuine connection. He was no longer seeking profit. He was seeking purpose.

And, for Leo Masters, that was the greatest return of all.

Chapter 11: The Silver Lining Trade

Leo Masters had been a shrewd investor for as long as he could remember. From real estate to stocks, every cent he'd put forth was calculated with razor-sharp precision. Watching his investments blossom and yield returns had always been his pride and joy. But now, his most recent investment—the community center renovation—had a different feel entirely. He hadn't invested for profit this time; he'd invested to make a difference.

And as it turned out, that difference was beginning to show.

It all started with a text message from Frank, the director of the community center, about a month after the renovations were complete. The message was brief but filled with excitement:

"Leo! Incredible turnout at the center this weekend—basketball courts full, dance classes packed, the cafe is buzzing! Couldn't have done this without you!"

Reading the message, Leo felt an unexpected warmth fill him. Just months ago, he would have viewed that turnout in terms of profits—ticket sales, concessions, memberships. But now, he was just... proud.

The community center had become a hub, not only for activities but for friendships, family gatherings, and after-school programs. Children who had nowhere to go before were now spending their afternoons in dance or sports classes. Older folks enjoyed social hours and pottery sessions. And families came in droves, attending workshops, movie nights, and even the occasional talent show.

Leo began visiting the center regularly, often slipping in unannounced and blending into the background as he observed people enjoying the space he'd helped revitalize. He watched as parents laughed, kids played, and seniors exchanged stories. And with each visit, he felt something inside him loosen, as if he'd been carrying a weight he'd never even noticed until now.

But as the center thrived, an old part of Leo—the strategist, the entrepreneur—began to creep back in.

It started innocently enough. One Saturday morning, Leo arrived at the center to find a line forming outside. People were waiting for one of the new pottery classes that had become incredibly popular, and as he scanned the queue, an idea formed.

He chuckled to himself. "If we had a VIP line with premium memberships, we could increase class capacity and even start branded merchandise sales for the kids' programs."

Then, a moment later, he cringed. *What am I doing?*

Pushing the thought away, he continued inside, determined to enjoy the success without turning it into an enterprise. But the urge persisted, and with each new success the center experienced, his mind returned to how he could "maximize returns."

The café, for instance, was always packed with people ordering coffee and snacks. Leo found himself mentally mapping out ideas for a loyalty program, a menu expansion, and even the prospect of selling reusable cups with the community center's logo. It took all his willpower to refrain from sharing these "strategies" with Frank.

Yet, as he observed the community embracing the center in its natural, unembellished state, Leo began to see the humor in his instinct to monetize everything.

One day, he even laughed out loud, earning a confused look from a nearby volunteer. Here he was, battling his own subconscious to keep his fingers off the profit buttons, like some kind of reforming workaholic trying to resist the allure of a spreadsheet.

As the weeks went by, Leo noticed how the community itself was taking the lead in driving new initiatives. Parents began volunteering to run extra classes, local artists offered workshops for free, and teenagers stepped up to help with after-school programs for younger kids. Each time someone came forward, Leo felt that familiar tug to organize it, streamline it, make it... efficient.

But he resisted, instead deciding to let the community shape the center's activities on their own terms.

One Friday afternoon, Leo was chatting with Grace, a regular at the center and an old friend he'd met during his early days volunteering. Grace had become somewhat of a guide for him, helping him understand the nuances of kindness, generosity, and community.

"The café's busier than ever," Leo said, trying to keep his excitement in check. "I could install a few more espresso machines, maybe add a second barista to speed things up."

Grace smiled knowingly. "Or… you could let people enjoy their coffee and the bit of extra time it takes. You know, slow things down. Gives people a chance to talk while they wait."

Leo stared at her. "But they could be served faster, Grace. They're standing there waiting. Efficiency!"

Grace's smile widened, and she chuckled softly. "Leo, not everything's about maximizing output. Sometimes, the waiting itself has value. People enjoy those little pauses, those moments to talk to their neighbors. It's the people and the atmosphere they come for, not just the coffee."

Leo felt a pang of realization. *People and atmosphere.* All his life, he'd thought of waiting as wasted time. But here, waiting was an opportunity—an opportunity to connect, to share, to breathe.

Then came the idea for the "Grand Opening Festival," a brainchild of some of the community center's volunteers. They envisioned an entire weekend of activities—games, live music, food stalls, crafts, and even a small talent show. When Leo first heard the plan, his initial reaction was one of skepticism. It sounded disorganized, and he half expected the event to be a mess.

But as the weekend unfolded, he watched with awe and amazement. The event was alive with energy. Children darted between stalls, families shared laughter over homemade treats, and friends clapped and cheered during the talent show. Leo even joined in for a round of musical chairs, earning a surprising amount of applause when he made it to the final two before dramatically falling over.

As he wandered the bustling center, he found himself marveling at what had taken shape. He had done nothing to orchestrate the festival, yet it had grown into something beautiful. The joy of the event was so organic, so genuine. For the first time, Leo felt the profound satisfaction of simply watching something flourish without needing to control it.

Later that evening, Leo stood on the balcony overlooking the festival grounds. Frank joined him, patting him on the back.

"Pretty amazing, huh?" Frank said, nodding toward the crowd. "Look at them—this place has become a second home for so many people."

Leo looked down, a swell of pride filling his chest. "Yeah, it's... something else."

Frank grinned. "People keep asking who helped fund all this. They'd love to thank the person behind it."

Leo shook his head, smiling. "No, let them just enjoy it. It's not about me."

It was true; he didn't need the acknowledgment. Seeing the center succeed was reward enough. It was a new feeling, this quiet pride—a far cry from the accolades, bonuses, or returns he was accustomed to. And as he stood there, watching the community celebrate, he realized he'd finally found something that money couldn't buy: fulfillment from giving without expecting anything in return.

Over the next few weeks, Leo continued to drop by the center, but his role had changed. He wasn't there to oversee or direct but simply to be part of it. He volunteered with small tasks, helped with cleanup after events, and even joined a book club that had formed among some of the regulars.

One afternoon, a young woman approached him as he was putting away folding chairs. She introduced herself as Anna, the mother of a boy who frequented the center.

"Thank you, Mr. Masters," she said, smiling. "I heard you were behind a lot of the work here. My son absolutely loves coming here—it's given him a sense of purpose, somewhere he feels he belongs."

Leo smiled, his chest tightening slightly. "I'm glad he enjoys it. That's what it's all for."

She hesitated before adding, "I know you're a businessman, so this may sound silly, but... the real value of what you've done here isn't just in the building or the renovations. It's in what you've given to the community. And that kind of wealth? You can't measure it in dollars."

Leo's heart felt light. For years, his life had been about transactions, about value measured on a spreadsheet. But here, in this community center, he'd discovered a wealth beyond profit.

That night, as Leo lay in bed, he found himself smiling. He thought back to his initial spreadsheets, his awkward attempts at kindness, his endless calculations of "returns" on things that didn't need to be quantified.

He realized how much he had changed. He no longer felt the need to own or control every detail. He didn't feel the itch to capitalize on every opportunity or turn every gesture into a business proposition. Instead, he was learning to appreciate the intrinsic value of things—the laughter, the camaraderie, the bonds he'd formed.

This journey had started as a way to escape the tedium of his success, but it had become a pathway to something deeper, something that didn't fit on any balance sheet.

In the months that followed, Leo continued to invest his time at the center, growing closer to the people there and experiencing more joy than he'd ever known from his former pursuits. He was learning to let go of the need to quantify everything, finding comfort in the knowledge that some things didn't need a bottom line to be worthwhile.

And for Leo Masters, that was the most profound silver lining of all.

Chapter 12: The Value of Nothing

Leo Masters was used to always having control—control over his finances, his time, and even the people around him. Yet, recently, he had discovered a surprising thrill in releasing some of that grip. The community center had taught him more than he ever expected about the rewards of giving without expecting returns, of watching something thrive simply because he'd helped it along.

Still, there was something nagging at him. Despite all the changes he had made in his life, Leo still relied on his wealth as a safety net. He was generous, yes, but only because he could afford to be. What would it be like to experience life without his usual resources? The idea both intrigued and terrified him.

One Thursday morning, after a conversation with Grace about the importance of simply being there for others, Leo decided he would spend the day "money-free." No credit cards, no wallet, no phone calls to his accountant. Just Leo, his wits, and whatever the day brought his way. He could already feel the discomfort brewing, but he pushed it down. *How hard could it be?*

Leo stood in his kitchen, staring at his abandoned wallet on the counter as if it were a lifeline. He gave himself one last pep talk. "Alright, Leo, you can do this. Just a day without money. People do it all the time!"

After a deep breath, he stepped out the door, leaving his car keys behind too. It felt strange, almost like he'd forgotten part of himself. He had no idea what he'd do all day, but maybe that was the point.

It was a short walk to the community center, where he figured he could help out without needing to spend anything. Along the way, he found himself hyper-aware of every store, restaurant, and service, each one a reminder of the conveniences he usually took for granted. His stomach growled, and he sighed, realizing he'd forgotten breakfast. *Well, this is off to a great start.*

By the time he arrived at the community center, he'd already checked his pockets for his wallet three times, only to remember with each pang of panic that he didn't have it. Stepping into the bustling center, Leo scanned the room for Grace. If anyone could guide him through his day "off the financial grid," it was her.

He found her in the café area, setting up chairs for a morning yoga class. "Grace," he said, approaching her with what he hoped was a casual smile, "I'm trying something new today. Going the whole day without money."

Grace gave him an amused look. "No money? Not even a credit card tucked away somewhere?"

"Nope, not even my emergency card," he said, feeling oddly proud. "Thought I'd see what it's like to live without it, maybe try to help some people without just, you know, throwing cash at things."

"Well, Leo," Grace laughed, "I think you'll find there's plenty you can do for others that doesn't involve your wallet. Ready for your first assignment?"

Leo nodded, feeling a surge of excitement and apprehension. "Absolutely. What do you need me to do?"

She handed him a broom and pointed to the main hall, where decorations from a recent party were still hanging. "You can start by tidying up in there. Sometimes, the simplest acts are the most helpful."

Leo's excitement waned as he stared at the task in front of him. He couldn't remember the last time he'd held a broom. For a moment, he awkwardly maneuvered it, unsure how to even start. He looked around, feeling like a fish out of water, until a couple of teenagers passed by, stifling laughs as they watched him struggle.

"Need some help there, Mr. Masters?" one of them asked, grinning.

Leo straightened his shoulders, brushing off his embarrassment. "No, no, just... warming up."

As he swept the floor, he tried to focus on the rhythm, the back-and-forth motion, the gradual clearing of debris. It was simple work but oddly satisfying. For once, he wasn't thinking about profit margins or investments. He was simply cleaning, contributing to the community center's upkeep without fanfare.

By the time he'd finished, his hands were sore, and his shirt was smudged with dust, but he felt a strange sense of pride.

Just as Leo was getting ready to ask Grace for his next task, he heard raised voices outside. He peeked through the window and saw two men trying to change a flat tire on an old sedan. Neither looked particularly skilled at it, and from the frustrated expressions on their faces, Leo could tell they were out of their depth.

Without thinking, he rushed out to offer assistance. "Hey, need a hand?"

The older man looked at him in relief. "Yes, please. I haven't changed a tire in ages, and my son here—" he nodded toward the younger man— "he's never done it before."

Leo realized he'd never changed a tire in his life either, but he decided to give it a try anyway. Following a vague memory of a YouTube tutorial he'd watched years ago, he set to work. The process was messy, and he struggled to loosen the lug nuts, but with teamwork and a fair amount of fumbling, they managed to get the spare tire on.

The older man clapped him on the shoulder. "Thank you, young man. We'd have been here all day without you."

Leo smiled, feeling an odd warmth in his chest. Normally, he'd have just called for roadside assistance and sent them the bill. But being hands-on, even in a situation as mundane as changing a tire, felt unexpectedly fulfilling.

As the morning passed, Leo's stomach started to grumble again. He realized he had no money for lunch and no easy way to get food. For a moment, he considered heading home to grab his wallet, but he pushed the thought away, determined to see the experiment through.

Just then, Frank, the community center director, came by with a few extra sandwiches. "Leo, you hungry? I ended up with extras from a café order this morning. Feel free to take one."

Relieved, Leo took the sandwich with a grin. "Frank, you're a lifesaver."

He sat in the courtyard, unwrapping his lunch and savoring every bite. Normally, he would've paid no mind to such a simple meal. But now, eating this sandwich felt like a victory, a meal earned through his commitment to going without.

With a full stomach, Leo returned to the center, where Grace introduced him to an elderly man named Mr. Thompson, who had recently started coming to the center for companionship after losing his wife.

"Mr. Thompson just needs someone to talk to," Grace explained. "Sometimes, lending an ear is all someone needs."

Leo sat with Mr. Thompson, who shared stories of his life, his family, and his years as a small business owner. Leo listened intently, genuinely interested in the man's experiences. Every so often, Mr. Thompson would ask for Leo's thoughts, and Leo would respond, offering encouragement and sympathy.

By the end of their conversation, Mr. Thompson looked at Leo with gratitude in his eyes. "Thank you, Leo. Sometimes, talking to someone who actually listens makes all the difference."

For Leo, the exchange was humbling. He'd spent years of his life in meetings, giving commands, making decisions. Yet here he was, realizing that simply listening to another human being was perhaps the most valuable thing he could offer.

As the day wound down, Leo found himself walking home with a newfound sense of peace. He hadn't spent a penny, yet he felt wealthier than he had in years. There was something uniquely fulfilling about the experiences he'd had that day—the sweat of hard work, the satisfaction of helping others, the joy of sharing a conversation.

When he arrived home, he resisted the urge to reach for his phone or laptop. Instead, he simply sat in his living room, reflecting on what he'd learned. For so long, he'd equated his value with his wealth, but today had shown him that he could offer so much more—his time, his presence, his willingness to connect.

Leo's experiment was intended to last only a day, but as he sat in the quiet of his home, he realized that he didn't want it to end. Maybe, just maybe, he'd start setting aside one day each week to go without money, to remind himself of what truly mattered.

He had spent so much of his life chasing profits, amassing wealth, and securing his future. But today had taught him that sometimes, the greatest wealth was found not in what he owned or could buy but in the moments of connection, compassion, and presence he offered freely.

And in that revelation, Leo found himself richer than he'd ever been.

Chapter 13: The Real Estate of the Heart

Leo's transformation from self-absorbed tycoon to someone actively seeking connection had been gradual. Day by day, his view of what made him "wealthy" had shifted from stock portfolios and property lines to something infinitely harder to calculate yet far more valuable.

After his wallet-free experiment in Chapter 12, Leo's mind was buzzing with thoughts. He'd experienced joy in unexpected places and connections that couldn't be bought. And now, as he reflected on what he had once considered valuable, it dawned on him that maybe the *real* wealth in life was what he'd always brushed aside as "soft stuff"—friendships, community, trust. These weren't assets that could be measured in dollars or square footage, but he could feel they were worth more than his entire property empire.

Determined to explore this newfound perspective, Leo set out on a new venture—not in real estate or stocks, but in building something he now jokingly called "the real estate of the heart."

Monday morning arrived, and Leo was in his office, holding a notepad with a list titled "Emotional Investments" at the top, followed by bullet points like *Time, Compassion, Listening,* and *Presence.* He let out a chuckle as he realized he was trying to quantify the intangible, almost as if he were a stock analyst drafting a report. *Can't teach an old dog new tricks,* he thought, amused at how his corporate instincts kept creeping back in.

Determined to put his new plan into action, Leo decided he would make a list of ways he could "invest" in the people around him, starting with the community center and his newfound friends. Grace was top on the list, followed by Mr. Thompson, Frank, and the many people he'd met over his recent adventures. He chuckled as he labeled them his "Top Priority Connections," as if they were shareholders or VIP clients. *Well, who says emotional investments can't have a little organization?*

Leo's first stop was the community center, where he'd planned to meet Grace for coffee. He'd brought a notepad with him, eager to discuss a few ideas he'd had about a possible scholarship fund for underprivileged students in the neighborhood. But when he arrived, he found Grace setting up for a pottery class, her face a mask of concentration.

"You're looking very businesslike today," she teased as he approached her, motioning to his leather-bound notepad.

"Oh, this old thing?" he replied with a grin, waving the notebook. "I just thought I'd bring it along in case I get inspired." He paused, then added, "Actually, Grace, I wanted to talk to you about... you know, making a more *lasting impact* here."

Grace raised an eyebrow, her smile warm but curious. "You're not planning to turn this place into some sort of profit venture, are you?"

"Absolutely not!" he said quickly, almost affronted by the suggestion. "No, no, I'm done with that. I just... I want to help. In a real way. Maybe start a scholarship fund, or fund some creative projects, or something that could actually change lives."

She looked at him, nodding slowly, and he could see a spark of approval in her eyes. "I think that's a wonderful idea, Leo. But remember, sometimes it's not just about funding projects. Sometimes, the most meaningful contributions are the small, consistent acts of kindness."

Leo thought about that, the wheels turning. In his world, big meant better. A flashy fund, a groundbreaking project—those were what his business instincts leaned toward. But here, in this world of connection, perhaps something simpler could be just as powerful. "So, you're saying... small gestures over time?"

Grace nodded. "Exactly. Consistent kindness, being there for people, listening—that's how you make a real impact."

It's like building equity, Leo thought to himself. *A little bit at a time, over years.* He jotted down "Small Acts = Big Returns" on his notepad and underlined it, chuckling at the irony of still using business terms to process this shift.

Following his talk with Grace, Leo began to approach every encounter with this new philosophy in mind. Each person he met was no longer a potential deal but a *connection* to invest in. And as he continued, he noticed something remarkable: this "investment" wasn't just about his actions. It changed him, too.

Take Mr. Thompson, for example. Leo found himself stopping by the elderly man's house every other day, just to say hello and share a cup of tea. Each time, Mr. Thompson shared a new story from his past, and with each story, Leo realized he wasn't just being entertained—he was learning. Mr. Thompson had faced hardships Leo could hardly imagine and had found ways to navigate them with resilience and humor. It was like he was teaching Leo how to *invest in life itself*.

One day, as they sat together on Mr. Thompson's porch, Leo marveled at the value he felt in that moment, a value unmeasured by his usual financial tools.

"You know, Mr. Thompson," he said, shaking his head with a laugh, "I've spent my life investing in property, stocks, businesses. But nothing's ever felt as... worthwhile as this. I think I might be the richest I've ever been."

Mr. Thompson chuckled. "Funny how the heart's currency works, huh? You give it away, and somehow you get more."

Leo nodded thoughtfully. *The heart's currency*—now that was an investment he could get behind.

Inspired by his newfound understanding, Leo proposed a "Small Acts of Kindness" program at the community center. It would involve simple activities, like a gardening club, a weekly reading hour for local kids, and even a craft night where people could make gifts for each other. The idea was to create spaces where people could give without expecting anything in return, just as he had learned.

At first, he worried his business-minded friends would think he'd gone soft. And in a way, he supposed he had—but in the best possible way. Still, he kept a touch of his humor about it all, jokingly calling it "The Leo Masters Investment Plan, Version 2.0." When Frank asked him if he'd lost his mind, Leo just laughed and replied, "Only the part that thought money was everything."

As he watched the program take off, with more and more people joining each week, Leo felt a sense of pride he hadn't experienced before. He wasn't cashing in on his name or reputation. He was simply watching something grow, something that would thrive long after he was gone.

One afternoon, as he was working on a garden plot with some neighborhood kids, Leo was surprised to see an old business partner, Doug, stroll up to him with a baffled look.

"Leo?" Doug said, squinting as if he couldn't quite believe his eyes. "What on earth are you doing here? Gardening?"

Leo laughed, wiping his hands on his jeans. "Yeah, Doug. Gardening. Giving back. Living the dream."

Doug raised an eyebrow. "This doesn't sound like the Leo Masters I know. No seven-figure deals here?"

Leo shook his head. "Not here, no. But, funny enough, this feels richer than any deal I've ever signed."

Doug looked at him skeptically, clearly not buying it. "What's gotten into you, man?"

"Just a change of heart, Doug," Leo replied, smiling. "I realized that real wealth isn't about what you own, but about the connections you make, the lives you touch."

Doug's expression softened, though he still seemed baffled "Well, it's your money... or, rather, *not* your money, I guess."

"Exactly!" Leo grinned. "But listen, Doug. If you ever want to try investing in something intangible, come join us here. It's not exactly high-yield in the traditional sense, but it's got returns that last."

Doug chuckled, shaking his head. "You're a strange one, Leo. But... maybe I'll come check it out."

As the weeks passed, Leo continued pouring himself into his newfound "real estate of the heart." Each day brought new challenges, new opportunities to connect. And with every act of kindness, every conversation shared, every laugh exchanged, he felt his spirit growing richer. This new investment strategy was paying off in ways he'd never anticipated.

One evening, as he sat alone in his office, he looked around at the walls adorned with awards, certificates, and newspaper clippings detailing his business triumphs. In the past, he'd looked at these as symbols of his success. But now, they felt... hollow.

He pulled a box from the shelf and began packing the awards away, replacing them with photos of the community center, candid shots of Mr. Thompson, Grace, and the children in the garden. With each framed photo he placed on the shelf, he felt a deeper satisfaction than he ever had when cashing a check or sealing a deal.

Leo took a deep breath and smiled to himself, the weight of superficial success lifting from his shoulders. He had built empires before, but this—this was an empire that would last, one where the wealth he generated wasn't in stocks or property but in laughter, shared stories, and the gratitude of others.

And, as he locked his office that night, Leo realized that he'd finally built a legacy worth leaving behind—one rooted not in the value of land or the price of shares, but in the real estate of the heart.

Chapter 14: The Debt of Gratitude

Leo had never imagined that the quiet, steady investments he'd been making in people's lives would come back to him in a way that made him the subject of genuine, heartfelt appreciation. In his mind, he'd been doing small, decent things—nothing extraordinary. But today would mark an unexpected turning point, one where he'd feel the full impact of his transformation. As he opened the community center doors, he had no idea a few surprises—and some much-needed laughs—were waiting just on the other side.

Leo strolled into the community center like any other day, already running through his mental checklist. Today's list included fixing the broken coffee machine, helping Grace set up for the weekly reading club, and, he chuckled, completing his ambitious goal to "invest in human connections," which he'd scribbled in his planner with a smiley face next to it. But as he walked into the center's main room, he was surprised to see a group of people waiting for him, and by the looks on their faces, it wasn't for a friendly coffee chat.

"Leo!" Grace called out, a smile lighting up her face. "Glad you're here. We've got a bit of a... surprise for you."

The crowd, a mix of familiar faces and newcomers, beamed at him with a kind of admiration that left him feeling both elated and hilariously uncomfortable. *Hero* was definitely not a title Leo had ever associated with himself; he'd left that role to firefighters, doctors, or action movie stars. But now, as he stood there, it was clear that in his journey of quiet kindness, he'd become something of a local legend.

Frank, the cantankerous old neighbor who'd once looked at Leo as if he were about to snatch the community center away, was the first to step forward. Frank cleared his throat, shifting awkwardly as if he'd rather be anywhere else. "Alright, I'll start, though I'm not one for speeches."

Leo fought back a laugh, whispering to Grace, "Would you look at this? Frank doing a speech!"

Ignoring Leo's jab, Frank went on, "So, Leo... I just want to say, I know we started off on the wrong foot. Thought you were just some rich kid who'd come in here and start throwing money around to make himself feel important. But I'll be honest," he paused, scratching his head, "I was wrong."

The crowd murmured their support, and Leo felt a blush creeping up his neck. He tried to brush it off with a self-deprecating smile, but Frank continued.

"When you funded that little gardening project and encouraged me to teach these kids, well, that gave me something to look forward to." He gestured to the group of kids who were regulars at his gardening lessons, now beaming at Leo with wide eyes and proud grins.

"Frank, I'm the one who should be thanking you," Leo said. "You taught those kids more than I ever could. They've told me all about your expertise in composting!"

The crowd chuckled, but Leo noticed the gratitude in Frank's eyes. "Thanks, Leo," Frank said, a little gruffly, before stepping back into the crowd. Leo felt a swell of pride—not in himself, but in Frank's journey. It was as if he'd watched an old grumpy cactus bloom into a surprisingly compassionate gardener.

Next, a young mother and her two kids stepped forward. Leo recognized them immediately. The McCarthys were new to town, having moved from out of state, and hadn't known anyone when they arrived. Leo had met them during one of his early visits to the community center and had suggested they join the "Small Acts of Kindness" program he'd started, as a way for them to meet others and feel part of the community.

Mrs. McCarthy, holding her youngest daughter's hand, looked a bit teary as she faced Leo. "Mr. Masters," she began, her voice a little wobbly, "I don't know if you realize what a difference you've made to us. Moving here was hard on the kids; they left their friends and the home they knew. But thanks to you, they've made friends here, they've started feeling at home."

Her son, who looked about ten, piped up, "And I'm in the gardening club with Frank now! We planted a whole row of carrots!"

Leo gave him a thumbs-up. "I bet those carrots are going to be delicious. And who knew? A city boy like me might even get a taste for gardening."

The little girl giggled, clutching a small drawing she'd made. She held it up to Leo—a crayon sketch of him with a big smile, surrounded by flowers and kids. "Thank you, Mr. Leo," she said shyly, and Leo's heart melted right then and there.

He took the drawing, touched by the innocence of her gratitude. "You have no idea how much this means to me," he told her, giving her a gentle pat on the head. In that moment, he realized he'd never felt this level of satisfaction from any stock certificate or business accolade.

Just when he thought he couldn't possibly take any more of this "hero" stuff, Grace stepped forward, a warm smile playing on her face. Leo couldn't resist rolling his eyes with a grin. "Oh no, Grace—don't tell me I've inspired you, too," he joked.

But Grace's expression was serious. "Actually, Leo, yes, you have," she said. "You've taught me that people can surprise you. I didn't expect much from you when you first came to the community center," she admitted with a laugh. "I thought, here's another big shot who'll throw some money at us and call it charity."

Leo grimaced, remembering his corporate self-assuredness that had driven her crazy early on. "Fair enough," he said, laughing at himself.

"But you stayed, Leo. You didn't just drop in with a check and disappear. You committed to this community, and you showed us that kindness—real, enduring kindness—is about more than just money."

Leo's usual confidence wavered, and he scratched his head, trying to think of a witty comeback but finding himself at a loss. Grace continued, "You've reminded us that anyone can change if they have the courage to let go of their own walls."

This gratitude hit Leo harder than he'd anticipated, and he found himself struggling to speak. "Well... I... guess I should be thanking *you*, Grace. You've shown me more about this whole heart thing than anyone else," he said, awkwardly gesturing with a smile. The crowd laughed, and Leo tried to regain his composure by clapping his hands.

By now, Leo had heard from neighbors, kids, and fellow community members who'd benefitted from his influence and friendship, and each story made him feel a depth of happiness he'd never quite known before. But the funniest moment of all came when little Susie—a precocious six-year-old with an astonishingly frank attitude—walked right up to him, hands on her hips.

"So, Mr. Leo," she declared, looking him straight in the eye, "are you gonna be our superhero forever?"

The crowd burst into laughter as Leo, taken aback, raised an eyebrow. "Superhero? Me? I don't even have a cape!" he teased.

"But you don't need a cape!" Susie insisted, her brow furrowing. "You're the one who got us all together and helped people. You're, like, Super-Leo!"

Leo couldn't contain his laughter. "Well, Super-Leo does have a nice ring to it," he said, posing dramatically with his hands on his hips, to the crowd's delight. "I guess if that's what you all need, I'm here to serve!" He knew he'd never been called a hero or a superhero before, not in his corporate life, anyway. And while the whole idea seemed ridiculous, he had to admit—there was something incredibly freeing about it.

After the crowd began to disperse, Leo sat quietly with Grace, the weight of the day's gratitude finally settling in. He hadn't expected people to come back to him with stories of how his small acts of kindness had influenced them, and certainly not with this level of appreciation. He thought back to all those years of corporate successes, the awards, the high-stakes deals—none of it had ever come close to this. Here, there were no graphs to prove the returns, no spreadsheets to measure the impact, just a feeling, a deep and powerful sense of belonging.

"It's funny, Grace," he said, looking around at the community center and then back at her. "I spent my whole life thinking gratitude was a one-way street. People owed me because I gave them jobs, I made things happen. But... I guess I never understood that real gratitude goes both ways."

Grace smiled, nodding. "It's a debt we all carry with us," she said. "And it's not one you can pay off. It grows and grows, and the more you give, the more you receive."

Leo shook his head, laughing softly. "Well, looks like I'm in debt for life, then."

Grace laughed, too. "Aren't we all?"

As he left that day, Leo realized that this was the kind of debt he was proud to carry. He understood now that gratitude wasn't a transaction, but a bond, an unseen thread that connected him to those he'd helped and, in turn, bound them to him. It was something that, in his previous life, he'd missed entirely. And now, as he walked down the street, a sense of peace washed over him, knowing that his wealth was, for once, something real.

Chapter 15: The Final Investment

As the sun dipped below the horizon, casting a golden hue over the quiet town, Leo sat on a bench in the park, deep in thought. He hadn't come here to calculate profit margins or close another business deal; today, he was reflecting. His life had taken a radical turn, one that was once unimaginable. Here he was, Leo Masters—the former Wall Street hotshot, the guy who used to measure success in dollars and dividends—now a man who found purpose in the people around him.

When Leo had first invested in the community center and its people, it had been a tentative experiment, a trial run for his so-called "investment in humanity." He hadn't anticipated that each small step would bring him closer to a life so different from his previous one, yet so incredibly fulfilling. He chuckled to himself, marveling at the irony. The man who once thought he knew everything about making returns had stumbled upon the most valuable investment of his life, completely by accident.

He couldn't help but laugh, remembering his initial conversations with Grace and the townsfolk, where they'd eyed him with open suspicion. *Just some city guy with too much money*, he thought. *And now, here I am, the self-appointed "angel investor" of goodwill.*

As he looked around the park, Leo spotted faces that he'd grown to care about. There was Frank, the grumpy old gardener, now proudly instructing a group of kids in the fine art of composting. Not far away, Mrs. McCarthy and her kids were reading a book together on a picnic blanket, the little girl occasionally glancing over at him with a shy smile. Leo gave her a wave, and she beamed, waving back.

He thought back to the day when Frank had grudgingly thanked him for the gardening project, how the McCarthy family had shared their gratitude for his small acts of kindness, and the endless other people he'd helped in ways he never thought would matter. And each one of these memories carried something priceless—something that, no matter how vast his fortune, he could never buy: true joy.

In the beginning, Leo had been baffled by the way people responded to these small gestures. He hadn't realized it was possible to make such a difference with so little, at least financially. But as he'd discovered, the impact was huge in every other way. It wasn't the money; it was the time, the care, the encouragement he had offered. He realized that investing in human potential wasn't just about giving people resources; it was about showing them that someone genuinely believed in them.

For years, Leo had thought about his "legacy" in terms of financial empires and acquisitions. He'd imagined towers with his name on them, bank accounts bulging with figures no human could ever need. But this new version of his legacy was different—much softer and infinitely richer.

The thought came to him suddenly, as he watched the sun casting warm hues on the park. *What if I made this my life's work? What if I used my fortune to do something bigger than just making money?*

The idea was both exhilarating and a little terrifying. Leo had been in control of massive ventures before, but this...this was personal. His heart raced as the possibilities unfurled in his mind.

He could start by creating a foundation, one that provided resources and support for communities like this one. But he didn't want it to be the kind of foundation that simply handed out checks and called it philanthropy. No, this would be something much more involved—something that focused on empowering people to help themselves, the same way he'd done here in this town.

Excited, Leo set about planning his new venture with the same meticulous energy he'd once reserved for his Wall Street deals. He began scribbling down ideas in his notebook, each one grander than the last. The only difference was, these were ideas about creating opportunities for others, not just multiplying his own wealth.

The next morning, he walked into the community center with his plan. Grace, noticing his enthusiasm, quirked an eyebrow. "What's got you all fired up today, Mr. Masters?" she asked.

Leo grinned. "Grace, I think it's time I make my final investment."

She looked at him, mildly puzzled. "Final investment?"

He handed her his notebook, where he'd hastily sketched out his vision for a community-based foundation. "I want to take what we've done here and scale it up. Not just here, but in communities across the country. I want to build a foundation that focuses on investing in people—offering them resources, skills, and support to build their own futures."

Grace skimmed the notebook, her eyebrows shooting up in surprise. "Leo, this is...wow." She looked up, a genuine smile spreading across her face. "But are you ready for this? Philanthropy isn't exactly like trading stocks, you know."

"Oh, trust me, I'm aware," he laughed. "I've gotten pretty good at balancing kindness with reality, thanks to you."

He sighed, realizing he was now embracing the unpredictability of helping people. He couldn't calculate every outcome or predict every return. But that was part of what made this so beautiful.

Grace, touched by his sincerity, placed a hand on his shoulder. "You know, Leo, you may be the first philanthropist in history to make 'return on kindness' a thing."

Leo laughed. "Well, someone's got to try!"

Leo dove into his new project with his usual tenacity. The foundation, which he cheekily dubbed "The Masters of Purpose," quickly gained traction. Word spread about this eccentric ex-Wall Streeter turned philanthropist, and soon, communities across the state were reaching out for guidance, resources, and support.

The day of the foundation's launch event arrived, and Leo found himself in the middle of a crowd of smiling faces, shaking hands and answering endless questions. He had to admit, he felt like a bit of a fish out of water. Gone were the tailored suits and corporate jargon; instead, he was navigating an entirely new landscape of community leaders, local officials, and countless regular people who simply wanted to make their neighborhoods better.

One particular conversation stood out that day. A young man approached him, clearly nervous. "Mr. Masters, I just want to say that what you're doing here means a lot. I come from a neighborhood where nobody really gets a chance to make anything of themselves. Seeing you invest in people like us—it gives us hope."

Leo, who would have once brushed off such sentiments with polite detachment, now found himself deeply moved. "Thank you," he replied, sincerity radiating from his voice. "But honestly, you're the one doing the hard work. I'm just here to help you along the way."

The young man grinned. "Well, I'm glad you're here, Mr. Masters. You're showing people that even 'big shots' can care."

Leo chuckled. "I think I've officially retired from being a 'big shot,'" he replied, but his heart swelled with pride.

Over the following months, Leo's life settled into a new rhythm. He was no longer on Wall Street, calculating returns, leveraging buyouts, or leading takeovers. Instead, he was building something much more meaningful. The foundation wasn't just about giving money; it was about building skills, fostering connections, and empowering individuals to achieve their dreams.

Leo began traveling to different communities, sometimes meeting with city council members, sometimes working directly with individuals trying to start small businesses or support local initiatives. Every encounter enriched him, each person leaving their unique imprint on his life.

One memorable visit took him to a small town struggling to revitalize their main street. The community leaders shared their vision for a bustling, thriving town center, full of locally owned shops and cafes. Leo listened, nodding thoughtfully, and found himself mentally weighing the project's worth—not in terms of financial return, but in human potential.

"It's a big risk," he said, thoughtfully. "But honestly, some of the best risks don't have anything to do with profit margins. They're about making life better for people."

The team looked at him, surprised by his response, and Leo smiled. This was his new reality. He wasn't calculating dollars; he was calculating dreams, and the payoff was something money could never buy.

One evening, after a long day of meetings and plans, Leo sat alone in his new office at the foundation. The walls were lined with photos from various communities he'd helped, each one a testament to the work they'd done together. He leaned back, a sense of peace settling over him as he took it all in.

He thought back to his old life, his days of endless ambition and tireless pursuit of more. But now, he realized, he'd found a different kind of wealth—one that didn't diminish over time but grew with each person he helped, each life he touched.

It was funny, he thought, how the man who'd once prided himself on never leaving money on the table had found the greatest fulfillment in giving without expecting anything in return. In the end, his final investment wasn't in stocks or real estate; it was in people, in lives, in human potential. And that, he knew, was an investment that would keep growing long after he was gone.

As he locked up the office that night, Leo felt a deep sense of contentment. He no longer needed to prove himself or chase some elusive

Dear Readers,

As we reach the end of Leo Masters' journey, I want to take a moment to express my heartfelt gratitude to each of you. Thank you for joining me on this adventure, for allowing me to share Leo's story, and for embracing the themes of growth, connection, and the true meaning of wealth.

When I began writing this book, my intention was to explore the transformative power of human relationships and the joy that comes from investing in others. Leo's evolution from a profit-driven businessman to a compassionate philanthropist reflects a universal truth: that fulfillment often lies not in what we possess but in how we uplift those around us.

In a world where success is frequently measured in monetary terms, it's easy to forget the richness of human connection. Through Leo, I aimed to highlight that our most significant investments are those we make in people—the friendships we nurture, the communities we support, and the lives we touch with kindness.

As you reflect on Leo's experiences, I hope you find inspiration to seek your own path toward fulfillment. Whether through acts of kindness, volunteering, or simply being present for someone in need, each of us has the power to create change. You might discover, as Leo did, that the most gratifying moments often arise from the simplest acts of generosity.

I also want to thank you for your patience and understanding as I navigated this storytelling process. Writing this book has been a journey of self-discovery for me, reminding me of the importance of connection and compassion in our own lives.

Lastly, I invite you to carry Leo's lessons with you. Let us celebrate the power of community, the beauty of empathy, and the immeasurable value of giving without expectation. As you venture forth, may you find joy in the moments you share with others and discover that your greatest legacy will be the positive impact you leave on the world.

Thank you once again for being part of this journey. Here's to embracing the beauty of human connection and making meaningful investments in the lives of those around us!

With warm regards,

Smita Singh

Don't miss out!

Visit the website below and you can sign up to receive emails whenever Smita Singh publishes a new book. There's no charge and no obligation.

https://books2read.com/r/B-A-LYEOB-AZYDF

BOOKS 2 READ

Connecting independent readers to independent writers.

Did you love *A Heart's Investment - Beyond Billions*? Then you should read *The Mind's Trinity: Consciousness Subconsciousness Superconsciousness*[1] by Smita Singh!

What if the key to mastering your life lay within your own mind, waiting to be unlocked? Imagine, for a moment, that your thoughts were not just random, fleeting ideas but the product of a powerful team working behind the scenes to shape your reality.

At the forefront of your daily life is **Consciousness**—the constant stream of thoughts and decisions you are aware of. This is where you plan, react, and navigate your everyday tasks. It's the voice you hear most clearly, the part of you that interacts with the world. But beneath that, there's more.

---

1. https://books2read.com/u/m2azLd

2. https://books2read.com/u/m2azLd

Subconsciousness is the part of your mind that stores everything you've experienced, learned, and felt. Like a wise coach, it speaks to you in whispers, influencing your habits, reactions, and beliefs. Its power is often hidden, yet it's always working, helping you build and break patterns that define your life.

Beyond these two lies the often mysterious and deeply insightful **Superconsciousness**—a higher level of awareness that connects you to greater wisdom and purpose. Acting like a mentor, the superconscious mind doesn't just offer you solutions to problems; it gives you vision and insight, guiding you toward a deeper understanding of yourself and the world.

In this book, you'll follow Alex, a character who struggles with the chaos of everyday life, feeling lost and unsure of their direction. Through encounters with three inner guides—Connie (Consciousness), Subby (Subconsciousness), and Superna (Superconsciousness)—Alex embarks on a journey of self-discovery and inner mastery.

As you read, you'll not only witness Alex's transformation but also learn about your own mind's power. This story is both an adventure and a practical guide to understanding the forces within you that can help you lead a more fulfilled and purposeful life.

Get ready to meet your inner coach, mentor, and thinker, and begin your journey to mastering the mind!